A.F.K.

Where the Game Gets Real

J.M. Keller

ISBN: 978-0-9977913-1-0
ISBN: 978-0-9977913-3-4

CONTENTS

CHAPTER I

She drummed her fingers on the steering wheel and groaned as she looked at the miles of taillights that flowed like an angry red river in front of her. But this wasn't a river; rivers tend to move. "Goddamn, this traffic sucks," Nikki thought for the thousandth time as she allowed her car to creep another few feet closer to home.

The radio was on the all-news station, but there was no word yet of an accident up ahead, or any explanation at all as to why there was such a huge back up. No doubt she'd hear about it once she had already spotted the problem for herself and already knew what the fuck up of the day was on this miserable stretch of highway. Likely it was a fender bender, but everyone and their mother had to slow down and gawk at it. She had always hated it when people did that, but now she had her own reason to hate it even more.

Well, at least it wasn't snowing. When the road was the least bit wet, people around here just lost their minds and drove too slow or too fast and that always made for some amazing accidents. If it was snowing, well, screw that, she just wouldn't be driving. Not anymore. That's why God invented telecommuting. She yawned and drank some coffee as she thought sarcastically to herself, "God, I love my life."

A small smile of recognition graced her face. "Beginning to sound like your old self again, huh?" Then she sighed and lit a cigarette. Fucking traffic.

Doing a quick search through the radio stations proved once again nothing good was on, and still nothing informative either. Why is it that we have all these stations eating up bandwidth and not one of them plays a damn thing I want to hear except for traffic and weather reports? She nodded

1

in submission to herself. "Because you're getting old, that's why."

Thank God for her iPod. All the classics she loved were on there. It was just last week she heard Duran Duran playing on the Muzak system at the grocery store. Proof positive she was indeed getting old. She glanced at the clock in the dashboard, and saw she was definitely going to be getting late getting home. She reached for her cell phone, then her hand stopped. There wasn't anyone at home to call. There hadn't been for over a year now. She shook her head. Old habits, they die hard, don't they?

God, she still missed him. It didn't hurt like it used to when she thought about him. Now it felt more like just being stabbed in the gut, rather than having them all torn out and shredded while you watched. Yeah, big improvement. It was times like this when calling home was such a poignant memory; the simple ritual of a phone call to say you'd be late was now no longer required, but the urge to make that call never failed her. There was no one there waiting for her or worrying about her anymore. She slowly smiled with gratitude; that's not entirely true. She still did have friends that cared about her and cared very much if she was going to be late. Huffing in frustration she realized if the damn traffic didn't get moving soon, she'd have to give one of them a call.

She hadn't noticed during her introspection, but the traffic did seem to be picking up the pace. Thinking about Michael, she hadn't noticed the increase in speed. Clicking her teeth together in annoyance she chided herself aloud. "You need to be more careful; one day you're going to be doing that shit and not paying attention and get into an accident, too."
She snorted derisively. Being careful didn't help Michael. He was the most careful driver she knew. That truck driver was a careful driver, too, according to his driving and insurance records. That is, until he fell asleep at the wheel on the interstate during that morning rush hour. His truck crossed the median, hitting Michael's car head on and then taking out four more vehicles before it plowed into the woods alongside the road.

As she always did when she recalled that horrible moment, she offered up a small prayer that Michael didn't feel any pain before he died. Maybe if he was lucky, he didn't even see it coming. Well, she could hope. And the truck driver lived. Ain't that a bitch? She shook her head and willed herself to end this litany, or she'll be crying again before she got home.

Careful, girl. This all goes to show you being careful doesn't mean a damn thing. You can be as careful as you want, but it's always that other fucker you never saw coming that's going to come along and change your life for you. Seemed like a good rule to live by, and she adopted that philosophy as her own. If pressed, though, she'd deny it.

Some things always required being careful. Driving was one of them. Then there was her work. Not only the work itself, but also how she handled her colleagues. She sighed with resignation. Working kept her busy and paid her salary. She allowed herself another smile as she recalled the many ways she was different from most of her co-workers.

The smile broadened as she thought about Anna, particularly their last conversation, which had left Anna completely vexed, and herself thoroughly amused. That made her consider adopting another motto. Never try to explain gaming to a non-gamer unless you have a few hours to spare. She laughed as she remembered the look on Anna's face when she told her what she'd been furiously working on during her lunch break.

"Come on, let's go get some lunch, Nikki. One of these days you're going to turn into a can of soup if you don't eat something else."

"No, I can't," she frowned, tapping her pencil on the desk. "I have to get this DKP adjusted before tonight's raid."

Then she saw the look on Anna's face and wished she had lied and said she was working on her taxes.

"What? DKP? What the hell is that, a new stock index?"

Nikki laughed lightly. "No, nothing that complicated, although it can be a pain in my ass."

Anna was waiting as she always did, with that smile of hers and that patient look on her face. Ok, how do I blow through this explanation quickly? "DKP," Nikki began with the patience she reserved only for her best friend. "It stands for Dragon Kill Points. For every particular boss mob…err, big monster… we kill in the game, we are awarded a certain designated number of points called DKP. It's like credit or money."

She gestured with her pencil at a chart that was up on one of the monitors at her desk. "You keep track of those points, and if the boss your guild just killed drops an item you want, you bid on it, like an auction, using that DKP you've earned just like money."

Anna looked amused. "Boy, don't you wish they would implement something like that around here?" Anna could always make her laugh, and Nikki chuckled on cue.

"Yeah, it would sure make things more interesting."

Anna looked like she was considering her next question, then her face took on a look of understanding. "Oh, I remember now. This is for that game you play online, isn't it?"

Nikki nodded as she scanned her points chart again.

"Seems like a lot of work to put into a game."

"Yeah, it can be, but it pays to keep track as you go along. Tends to keep the bitching down to a minimum."

Anna sat down, lunch temporarily forgotten, and looked at the spreadsheet Nikki was updating on one of her monitors. She frowned and pointed to a phrase she saw there. "AFK." Anna tapped the screen with a fingernail. "What does that stand for?"

Nikki blinked at Anna to see if she was kidding. Nope, she wasn't. "Seriously?"

Anna nodded; her face shrouded with innocence.

"AFK stand for away from keyboard. You type it, or you can say it into your mic. It means you're going to be away from your keyboard, and hence your computer, so you'll be non-responsive. In this particular case," Nikki tapped the screen herself, indicating two names on the raid list, "These two folks were afk when we downed that boss, so, no points for them. You have to actively help take down the boss to earn the points."

Anna gave her the deer-in-the-headlights look. "Ok. So, right now, I'm afk."

Nikki smiled. "Correct."

"But you're not afk." Anna gestured to Nikki's keyboard.

"That, too, is correct. Very good, noob, you're catching on quick."

Anna narrowed her eyes. "Ok, smartass, what's a noob? Wait, never mind, it can't be good whatever it is."

Nikki chuckled and played with her pencil, twirling it like a baton through her fingers, not even gracing it with a look. "How about you go Google that one, Anna?" Nikki said evenly. "That is, if you can even spell Google."

Anna snorted and looked insulted. "I don't have to spell it, I have it on my toolbar."

Nikki rolled her eyes, and then Anna pointed at Nikki's pencil twirling around her fingers. "I hate it when you do that."

Nikki didn't miss a beat. With a quick flick of her wrist the pencil disappeared upwards.

Anna looked up and saw there were about 40 pencils above their heads; all of them impaled by their points into the dropped ceiling tile over her friend's desk. Anna chortled appreciatively. "I thought you only did that when you were annoyed at the Department?"

"No," Nikki deadpanned, "just annoyed, period."

Anna gave her a dirty look, then she ventured cautiously, "So, you're playing again, are you?"

Nikki nodded and finished looking at the figures on the website that was still up on her monitor.

"Well, good for you. Personally, I never understood how you could look at computers all day and then go home and play a game on them all night."

Nikki tapped the monitor with yet another pencil that came from her bottomless supply. "It's not about the computer, Anna, that's just a tool. It's what you do with it that's different from work. There's people I play with…"

Rolling her eyes, Anna then gave Nikki a long-suffering look.

"Yes, real people, Anna. That's what makes it different, the interaction with them. It's challenging, thought provoking, and hell of a lot of fun."

Anna looked resigned, then she sighed and reached over to pat Nikki on her wrist. "You always did enjoy that, and it's about time you did something you enjoyed again. Why did you stop playing?"

Nikki looked up at Anna quickly, then at the picture of Michael that was still on her desk next to the pictures of her two daughters.

Lowering her voice and with a touch of sadness, Nikki made herself reply.

"He played too, Anna, every night, just like I did. Same game, same people. People that knew us both, as a couple. That made it hard…"

Anna stood up and looked out the window at the rain.

Nikki stood up too, reaching for the ever present can of soup in the cubbie above her desk.

Anna sighed and shook her head. "I just don't understand what you get out of playing this game. Being up all hours and doing things that never seem to end. There's no real winner, and now it looks like there's actual work involved, too. How is that fun?"

Following her friends gaze, Nikki looked out the window, too, thinking the rain was going to make the drive home a tough commute.

"If memory serves," Anna softly added. "A lot of these people you play with, you've known for years, right?"

Nikki nodded silently, still looking at the rain.

"And some of those people, you must also really consider them to be your friends, huh?"

Nikki smiled, and nodded again. Maybe there was hope for Anna after all.

Anna started to move down the hallway. "Friends are good for you, Nikki, if you'd give them the chance. Are you playing tonight?"

Feeling somewhat guilty, Nikki smiled. "I hope to, if I get home in time."

Anna made note of the real smile that surfaced on her friend's face, then she smirked and walked off back down the hallway. "I saw that," she said over her shoulder. "Better be careful. For a minute there, you almost looked happy. Put that damn soup away; I'll grab you some real food while I'm out. And good luck with your DKP, or PKU, or whatever the hell it is you're fiddling with…" As Anna disappeared down the hallway, Nikki smiled fondly at her. Yes, maybe there was hope for her, after all.

Nikki grinned to herself as she eased her car forward in the snarled traffic again. She knew Anna tried to understand, but unless you played, you just weren't a part of that world. As she stole a look at the clock on her dashboard, it reminded her she was going to be late. She reached for her cell phone again, but this time the gesture came with ease.

Pressing a speed dial number, she waited through the rings, but then got voice mail. "Bullshit, where the hell are you?" Nikki muttered under her breath. She tried another number. Busy. Then another one. Busy. Busy? What the hell? Must be the weather screwing up the signal. She dropped her cell into the cup holder on her console with a bit of annoyance.

"Hell, it doesn't screw up often enough to get angry about it, but dammit, why tonight?"

Cursing her luck and discount cell phone service providers in general, Nikki pondered who she could call next. Before she decided, her cell phone began to play a familiar tune and she grinned fondly. Adam was calling her back.

Hitting the button on her steering wheel, she answered the call. "Hey, how ya doing, Adam?"

"Not bad. Stuck in traffic, are you?"

"How did you guess?"

"I saw you called. That's the only time you call me."

"That's not true!"

"I know," he chuckled softly, and Nikki could hear the teasing lilt in his voice as he started in on her. "Don't go ballistic on me. When I answered and I couldn't hear anything, I figured it must be something with the phone, or a tower, or some other technological screw up, so I called you back."

"Well, I'm glad you did. It's raining like a bitch and nothing on the road was moving. I'm going to be a little late. I'm past the worst of it, but it's still gonna be a while. Tell folks I'll be there, but if they have to give away my spot, its ok."

"No, it isn't. You can't help the traffic. It's not like you're one of those no-show losers we have to deal with."

Nikki could hear Adam typing in the background. "Ok, done. The ones who are on now, know you're delayed. And we'll tell the rest as they log on. See, no worries."

"Well thank you, as usual."

"What, are you kidding? We're all glad to see you're raiding again. We missed you, girlie." Then there was a pause. "I missed you."

Nikki smiled a sad smile and was glad no one could see her face right then. She tried to talk, but the words just didn't come out. Adam picked up on the silence and patiently waited.

Finally, Nikki broke the silence. "I'm so far behind, Adam, I'll never catch up with you guys now."

"Pffft, who gives a damn about that?" he countered with annoyance. "You will get caught up eventually. That's what guildies are there for. We'll get you caught up in a few weeks, tops. Guaranteed."

She smiled at the easy assurance in her friend's voice. "Ok, if you say so; thy will be done."

Adam laughed lightly. "Damn right, and don't you forget it."

She saw her exit was coming up and as much as she didn't want to stop talking, knew she had to get off the phone. "Ok, I'm not far out now, I have to run in and do all that girl stuff I need to do, then I'll be in as soon as I can."

"Alrighty, we'll be waiting. Like always. Talk to you soon."

Nikki wasn't aware that she was smiling. "Ok, and thanks! Be there soon! Bye."

Hanging up, she didn't bother with the radio again. She was almost home now. There was no problem merging as she left the exit ramp off the interstate. By now most of the traffic near her home had thinned out. Trying to remember the forecast for tomorrow morning, she decided she better fill up with gas now.

As the gas pumped into the tank, she rolled her eyes and bit her bottom lip. Gonna be even later, she thought, but better late for the raid than late for work in the morning. A smile tugged at the corner of her mouth as she thought how that explanation would go over with her guildies. Better them, she thought wryly, than her boss.

Driving toward home, she decided the extra five minutes it took her to get home weren't worth mentioning. She pulled up in front of her house and parked. She grabbed her briefcase and ran through the rain to get inside.

Running into the kitchen, she put her briefcase down and opened it, took out her work cell phone and plugged that and her personal cell into their chargers. Then she ran upstairs into the bathroom and starting the water running in the sink, so it'd warm up. She took off her suit and hung it up, then ricocheted back into the bathroom to wash the makeup off her face and brush her teeth. Then she threw on a tee shirt and some sweatpants and sprinted downstairs to the computer room, grabbing an apple on the way. She'd eat later.

As her gaming computer was booting up she went into the

laundry room and threw a load into the washer then raced back up the stairs, back into the computer room. Welcome to the life of a gamer, Nikki thought with a bemused smile and wondered what Anna would say if she saw her charging around like a maniac when she got home instead of plopping on the couch with a glass of wine. How boring, she thought, as she grabbed her mouse and double clicked the icon on her desktop to enter the game.

Up came the splash screen and she logged in. Woot! No queue to log in tonight. She ran into the kitchen and grabbed a bottle of water from the fridge, then back down the hall she went. Sitting down in front on her computer, she grabbed her headset and draped it around her neck and moved the mic where it needed to be to pick up her voice. She didn't like having the headset on over her ears when she was alone, so she used the computers sound system instead of the headphones. She double clicked the icon for the voice communication software, and then logged into their guild's chat channel.

She heard the voices of her friends filtering into the room through her speakers and she grinned. The warm feeling reminded her of walking into her Mother's house for Thanksgiving dinner. She heard the voices of people she loved, and it warmed her heart, but sweet Jesus, what a pain in the ass they could be at times. The analogy was perfect. These people were just like family.

Nikki sighed and took a drink of water. Most of the folks in her guild were men but let a raid start forming and they all became more like a bunch of whining PMS ridden women.

Time to strap on her attitude. Waiting until there was a lull in their conversation, she announced her presence with both a greeting and an insult to the men. "Good evening, ladies." You can't help but smile when thirty or so people say hello to you all at once, even if you can't make out what each of them say.

"Hey, there she is!"
"Heyas!"
"Hey, Shylock"
"Shy, good to see you"
"About fuckin' time, noob."
She laughed out loud at that one.
"What's up byatch?"
"We waited for her? Shit…"
Yeah, the teasing was just beginning, making her feel welcome.
"Good evening, ma'am"
"Shy, how ya been?"
"Oh my God, is that Nikki?"
"Who the hell is Nikki?" She grinned; must be someone new.

Nikki had been playing this game a long, long time; even was a beta tester for it. She'd met quite a few of these guys personally, some on several different occasions, and there were also a few that she knew very well but still never had gotten the chance to meet them. They were so interesting, all different types of people and all with their personalities and quirks. Sometimes working with them ingame was like herding kittens, but more often than not they worked like a well-oiled machine. When that happened, it was so worth the effort. This game could be a blast if you didn't take all the crap that came with it too personally.

She saw her list of characters, her 'toons', come up on screen, and she chose her main character, a shaman named Shylock. As she entered the game, the invitation for the raid hit as soon as the screen focused, and she smiled. Man, it was good to be playing again. The hellos that were typed in the guild chat channel came next, along with the things some folks chose to type rather than say aloud in Ventrilo; often it was funnier that way. She replied to each of her greeters in turn, joking and laughing with them, doling out good-natured insults and taunts and generally giving as good as she got.

In guild chat, the guild leader announced he wanted to have a meeting this week, and he was asking when a good night for everyone was to attend online. Folks made their replies, and she took notes.

"I may have to go out of town on business Tuesday," Nikki told the group. "But I can do Monday."

She instantly got a private message ingame from Adam. "Where are you going?"

She smiled as she typed her reply. "Denver." He lived in Denver. She thought about it a moment, then typed to him again. "I'll be there a couple of days. Want to get together for dinner?"

His response was instantaneous. "Sure, I'll be around then. Give me a call when you get into town. Sounds like fun."

Nikki had thought of getting together before but didn't get the chance to ask until now. She felt strangely happy about him agreeing, too. "Will do," she dutifully typed back.

This was great! Adam was one of the people that she had known for years. In fact, he probably was her closest friend in game. She thought about that a moment. No, no qualifiers. He was a dear friend, period.

She smiled to herself, remembering fondly that some of these people really were her dearest friends. Many had actually come to Michaels's funeral. Adam couldn't make it. He told her he had issues at work, and he really tried but he just could not get away. Well, maybe that was true. He did live a long way off. It's not as though she had asked anyone to come, she wouldn't do such a thing. She smiled softly as she remembered some of these nuts that came to the funeral also lived a long distance away, but not as far away as Adam did.

More than anyone else though, these 'nuts' as she fondly thought of them had often called to check up on her through the days and weeks that slowly turned into months after the accident. However, out of the whole bunch, Adam took the cake. He had called at least once a day, usually more often, asking things like if she remembered to eat, pay the bills, do paperwork, was she sleeping, and all sorts of things she was not paying attention to without a nudge here and there. For a while, she began to think he was a royal pain in the ass, but as time passed, she saw it for what it really was; real concern for a friend.

She blinked and dragged herself back to the here and now. Time to pay attention. In the game, everyone was heading their toons to a rendezvous venue to gather before the raid. She typed into guild chat, "Ok, I'm on my way." Then she remembered she hadn't had time to use the bathroom yet. She typed, and also said into her mic, "Damn, I have to bio, afk." She ran upstairs to the bathroom. As she left the room, she heard a deadpan voice over the speakers that she knew all too well say, "Some things never change." Folks online laughed and so did she. Yeah, she missed this; she missed them. It was good to be back.

Tuesday morning came quickly. She got up at 5am and got dressed. All the packing was done the night before, and later than she would have liked it to be because of the guild meeting the night before. It takes a disciplined guild to play that game to get the results they all wanted, so if it cost a few hours of sleep, so be it, she temporized as she got ready. She told herself at least she could sleep on the plane. She chuckled, yeah like she ever slept on a plane anymore.

After taking one last walk through the house, making sure everything was turned off and put away, Nikki then put her two bags and her briefcase in the car. It was times like this she wished she had a laptop that had the capability to handle the game. She was taking a laptop for work, but that was a piece of crap compared to a gaming rig. It'd be so great to be able to play at night in the hotel room, but a laptop of that caliber was a luxury that she couldn't justify. Still, it was annoying. Everything is more annoying at this hour of the morning. She wondered if Adam would let her come over and use one of his computers while she was there so she wouldn't miss raiding at night. Then she wondered if she'd have the balls to ask him.

She stopped at the grocery store and went inside. She got cash from the ATM machine, bought two bunches of flowers and a bottle of water. She paused and wondered if there was anything she forgot, then she got in line and checked out. Walking back to the car, she noticed it was getting foggy. Joy. As if her destination needed the extra gloom factor.

It took just a few minutes to drive to the cemetery, and she drove without the radio on. It was going to be a warm day. It was already humid as hell and the fog just added to the soupy atmosphere. She pulled onto the cemetery road, turned right and up the narrower road to the eastern side. That all too familiar feeling of dread started to well up inside her. She drove slowly until the road bent to the right, then she pulled over and parked. Picking up the bunches of flowers, the bottle of water, and her keys, she locked the car, and stood there a moment.

Nikki sighed, and arranged the two bunches of flowers into one larger bunch. "Why do I always feel so damned uneasy when I'm here?" she thought once again, as she always did when she was here. She walked slowly toward the black marble headstone she knew so well, her heart feeling heavier with each step forward. Her emotions ebbed out and swirled around her, blending with the morning fog. God, she hated coming here, but she had to; she needed to visit Michael.

Nikki usually came to the cemetery on the weekends because it took so damn much out of her. It still hurt, she noticed, but not with the same sharpness and bite. She wondered if she should feel guilty about that. She bent down and put the flowers in the vase at the base of the headstone, and then opened the bottle of water and filled the vase. The ground was soaked from the morning fog, so she wouldn't be sitting down to talk to Michael this time, but she knew he'd understand. She put her hand on the cold black granite and spoke softly.

"I can't go to the airport with my dress soaking wet, can I, darling?"

She closed her eyes, ran her hand slowly over the incredible cold smoothness of the front of the headstone, and then traced her hand back up until her fingers touched the roughened edges on the narrower sides. She imagined just how he might answer that question, but she found no satisfaction in that and sighed heavily. She opened her eyes slowly and said very softly, "I wish you could answer me."

"He will one day."

Nikki jumped and spun around. Behind her was a familiar, wizened old man whom she had seen here before, but he had never spoken to her. Her heart was pounding in her throat. She didn't expect anyone else to be here this early and he scared the hell out of her.

"Forgive me, young lady, for intruding. I didn't mean to frighten you," the old man said as he took off his hat and gave her an apologetic look. He walked with difficulty toward her, his crooked legs slowly moving him forward. "I thought you might have heard me walking up. Since I scared the bejesus out of you, the least I should do is introduce myself."

His pale blue eyes twinkled as he held out his hand, his arm shaking a bit with his infirmities. "The names Hodges, Everett Hodges."

"Mr. Hodges, good morning." Taking his frail hand in her, she shook it carefully. "I'm Nikki Anderson."

The old man glanced at the headstone and smiled, making Nikki wince. The engraving on the headstone seemed to make the relationship there obvious.

"Pleased to make your acquaintance, Ma'am. I've seen you here quite a bit, you know. Usually on the weekends, eh?"

Nikki nodded, watching the old gent with interest.

"That's always good, remembering to pay your respects."

"Yes sir." she said respectfully, and cautiously.

"I don't usually come out here this early, but I have to go get some tests done, so I thought I'd drop by and visit the ol' lady while I could." He gestured at a tombstone a few rows away. "I lost my wife thirty years ago to cancer, and I still come here at least once a week." Then Mr. Hodges cracked a small grin and winked. "That's about as much as we spoke when

12

she was alive, anyway, so why change things now?" The old man giggled at his own joke and Nikki smiled at his gallows humor.

Then the old man was looking down at the grass, looking for something. "Like I said before, I didn't mean to intrude, but I did hear what you said. Sounds, they carry farther in the fog, you know."

She nodded. My God this is weird, she thought, running into someone out here at this hour, and he feels compelled to be chummy, too.

He shuffled his feet and moved a bit to the side, bent down and pulled up a dandelion, found another and did the same. Then he slowly straightened up. "What I said before, about him answering you one day. He will, young lady, most assuredly he will. It may not be his voice you'll be hearing. May not even be him speaking at all. But one day, somehow, somewhere, he will answer you. I know what he'll say, too."

Nikki tilted her head and Mr. Hodges smiled the sage smile that only age and experience allows. "What he'll tell you is, go on with your life."

She blinked and felt like she'd had the wind knocked out of her. She thought morosely to herself, "My life? I'm alive, and he's not. Do I even have a life anymore?"

Noticing the stricken look on Nikki's face, Mr. Hodges felt compelled to confirm it. "It's true, for sure." Nodding for emphasis, Mr. Hodges turned and looked at the gravestone, then back at her. He bent over again in his quest for dandelions and spoke in a gentle grandfatherly tone. "Ms. Anderson, do you think being alone is what your Mr. Anderson would want for you? Do you think he would want you to stop living your life here with the living, because his life on this earth had ended?" He shook his head, as if fondly admonishing a misbehaving grandchild. "Ma'am, if he loved you, would he want you to live out the rest of your days here on Earth being unhappy? Of course, he wouldn't."

He gave her a smile and then Mr. Hodges then began to shuffle off, back down the hill through the damp grass to the road. As he walked away he called out a goodbye, "Was nice meeting you, ma'am. Try to have a good day, now." Then he stopped and turned around and looked right at her. "Try to have a good life."

Nikki watched as he turned and walked down to the street. She saw him get into a car that was waiting for him, and then it drove slowly away into the fog. Turning back to the gravestone, she shook her head and let out her breath. She hadn't realized she had been holding it while he was speaking until then.

She had to go. Kissing her fingertips and placing them gently on the engraved name of her husband, she silently said goodbye. The stone felt cold, damp and unyielding. So unlike Michael. Before she was consumed by sadness, she turned and walked slowly away.

.

CHAPTER II

Standing in the middle of the living room in a large and well-appointed apartment, self-absorbed and agitated, Nikki looks like she's about to jump out of her skin. The steady light from the lamp on the end table blends with the flicker and glow from the city's nightlights, playing across her features as she stares out the window. She has an empty pack of cigarettes in her left hand, alternately squeezing and releasing her grasp on it, making soft cellophane crumpling noises. It's late into the night, but she is fully dressed.

He isn't. No longer asleep, he rolls over and out of the bed in one fluid motion. Casting a glance first in the direction of the bathroom and seeing it empty, he next looks toward the living room and sees a light turned on. Silently, he walks slowly to the door.

Looking into the living room, when he sees her, his first reaction is the warmest of smiles. He becomes aware that she is dressed, and not in the type of clothes she would relax in, but the type of clothes she'd wear…to leave? His brow furrows with concern. His senses are jangling with alarm, but outwardly he remains quiet and composed. The tension her body is telegraphing fills the room with an almost palatable aura. Not all is well here.

Adam folds his arms across his chest and leans his shoulder on the doorjamb to the living room, unnoticed yet by Nikki. He is shirtless, his hair tousled but he did have the grace to pull on a pair of sweatpants before coming out of the bedroom.

He knows something's awry but has no idea what. He just hopes it wasn't something he did, or even worse, he hopes it wasn't what they both did a little while ago.

Hearing the faint sound of cellophane crinkling and seeing the empty cigarette pack in her hand, he figures he might as well start with the

15

obvious. He speaks quietly, hoping not to startle her. "If you're out of smokes, you're more than welcome to mine. I have plenty."

She quickly turns to face him; a nervous smile adorns her face. She shakes her head in the negative. Nikki looks down at the crumpled empty pack in her left hand, and then walks to the trash can under the computer table and throws it away with a bit more vigor than required. "I need to quit smoking these things anyway." She turns around and sees him still leaning on the doorjamb.

He watches her cautiously, and his eyes are full of concern. He doesn't know what this is all about, but he gets the feeling if he does or says the wrong thing, she's gonna bolt like a startled doe.

Nikki raises her hand and makes a dismissive motion. "It's ok. I have more in my bag. Enough to last until later today, anyway."

He shifts his weight from the door jamb back to his feet. "Which?"

Surprised, she gestures toward her bags. "The small one."

He turns around and paces to her luggage, drops to one knee and opens the small bag. He talks aloud as he digs inside. "Now if I know you...yup, right in the front...just like us smokers, always making sure the smokes are right where we can get 'em quick." He stands, turns, and walks casually toward her. "This is a good reason to quit! Because," He glances up at the clock and does a double take. "Good God, is it 3:30 in the morning?" Adam looks back at Nikki and frowns. "Even worse, there isn't a decent store around here that's open for hours. The only people outside right now are pill pushers, pimps, and prostitutes." Giving her a significant look, he tells her, "Not a place you need to be right now." He stops in front of her, and hands her the pack of cigarettes.

"Thank you." she says quietly as she reaches for them.

She grasps the pack gently, but he doesn't let them go. "What's going on?" Looking her up and down, he wordlessly remarks on her state of dress. With a questioning look on his face, he releases the pack of cigarettes and she takes them.

She turns and walks away from him, toward the window, then she turns and walks back towards him. "I came out here," she said to the floor, "because, because dammit, I just didn't know what to do!" Nikki looks up slowly, her words tumbling out in a rush. "I didn't know what you wanted me to do!" Pacing the floor, she gestures towards Adam as she speaks, "I didn't want to do the wrong thing, or be in the wrong place, or assume anything...oh, God, I'm not very good at this..." Nikki folds her arms across her chest and looks back out the window. "I don't know what the rules are... Christ, I never did."

Adam walks slowly over to stand in front of her, wanting to

calm her down. He hates seeing her this upset, especially when he doesn't think there's a reason. "Whoa, whoa…hey… hold on there." He steps closer to her and puts his hands on her shoulders. Smiling tenderly at her, he sees a tear slide down her cheek that she swiftly whisks away with her hand. He softly chuckles as he takes his right hand and gently wipes away another stray tear with his fingertips. "Hey, now. What in the world? What's this all about?"

Then suddenly a slightly horrified look spreads across his face. He grasps both her shoulders again and looks intently at her face. "Oh my God, I didn't hurt you, did, I?"

She blinks in surprise and glances up at him, her features clouded with exasperation. "What? Oh, Jesus, no. No. No, no, nothing like that. You didn't hurt me."

He visibly relaxes his shoulders and lets out a huge sigh. "Whew, my God, you gave me a fright."

She gives him a wry smile, then she mutters, "Not yet, anyway."

"Now, what's that supposed to…," Adam begins, but then stops as he decides against talking, thinking right now something unspoken might be best. "No, wait, wait a minute. Come here, come here, come here." Gently he folds her into his arms, holding her close to him but lightly, not wanting her to feel overwhelmed. Adam sighs deeply, smiling to himself. Softly into her ear he whispers, "I'll never understand how a woman that's smart as you are, can sometimes be so… be so silly."

Adam grins affectionately at her as his arms relax their embrace, and he places his hands back on her shoulders. Looking intently into her eyes, he sees the uncertainty she tries to hide. It only takes him a moment to decide what he needs to do next. "Listen, tell you what," he offers lightly, with an easy smile. "I'm going to go into the kitchen and make us some coffee, and you're going to go change into…," He shook his head, still not quite believing Nikki was in his living room. "Change into anything that's more comfortable than what you have on, and then, you and I, are going to sit down, and talk. How does that sound?"

She peers unbelievingly at him and whispers, "Fine, maybe… maybe we should. If you want to…"

He softly sighs and bows his head touching his forehead to hers. "I think the time has come for us to have a good, old fashioned, sit down, heart to heart." Gently he continued, his blue eyes glowing deeper in the subdued light. "No interruptions. No phone calls, no internet, no email. We'll have each other's undivided attention. God, did I just say that?"

She narrowed her eyes suspiciously at him, "You did, indeed, now if I can just hold you to that."

Huffing in mock offense, Adam chides, "Shush you, it was my idea."

Nikki throws him a dubious look over her shoulder as she walks through the doorway into the bedroom.

Walking into the small kitchen as she walks toward her bags on the bedroom floor, his mind goes over the events of the last few hours and the last several days. He smiles to himself as he grinds the coffee beans, but the smile is soon replaced by a contemplative look.

What can be bothering her? Things have been going wonderfully, but obviously something has her rattled. He fills the carafe with water, and starts to fill the coffee machine, but then pauses with the carafe in midair.

Oh, for God's sake, is that it? He pours in the water, now with a bemused look on his face. "Well, damn it, it's not like I did a very good job of telling her. No, I didn't tell her a damn thing, not what I should have. I know it must have shown, but, is she being so careful that she refuses to see the obvious?' Then he chuckles ruefully, but quietly so she can't hear him. "Careful? Look who's calling whom careful," he mentally asked himself. "And when has anything I've ever done been obvious?" Sighing, Adam turns on the coffee machine. "Ok, then. It's time to put her doubts to an end."

Trying to lighten the mood a bit, he starts talking to Nikki from the kitchen. "You know, the great thing about a place like this, is all I have to do is turn around, and I can see right into the bedroom."

She laughingly answers his suggestion. "Too late."

He looks around, sees her walk into the living room, and exclaims, "Dammit!" but with a smile on his face.

Nikki had already slipped into a tank top and short set, the kind made of soft touchable knit. Grinning, he walks out of the kitchen, grabs a T-shirt off the back of the couch and pulls it on.

Looking at the living room, he puts his hand on his chin, considering his options. "Ok, now, how should we...., ok, I'll sit here on the couch." Gesturing at the furniture, he's giving seating assignments. "You sit there on the loveseat so we can see each other, like that's hard to do in this place. No point getting a crick in our necks, though."

They both start to sit down, but then Adam jumps up. "Oh, wait wait wait, I forgot." He walks quickly over to Nikki, and pulls her into his arms again, and gives her a kiss.

She blinks at him and tentatively smiles up at him. "Good morning to you, too."

18

He gives her a slightly admonishing look. "Ahh, not bad, but we'll work on that though. I've always said, never start the day without a kiss good morning. That is, when and where that's feasible. Now where were we, oh yes, me on the couch and you on the loveseat over there."

They both sit in their appointed places. The couch and loveseat are facing each other with a small coffee table in between them. Not far apart at all, but apart enough to give her some space. She realizes what he's up to and gives him a bemused smile.

Settling into position, making a slightly exaggerated show of being prepared to sit there for however long this may take, Adam is now ready. With a serious, but quiet tone, he begins. "Now, for our first talking point. You said, "I didn't know what you wanted me to do." His eyebrows raise, wordlessly asking for a reply. Clearly, the floor is now all hers.

Nikki sighs and looks embarrassed. To Adam, she looks irresistibly cute, but he knows he can't say that. Yet. After a moment of uncertainty and looking at the floor, finally Nikki raises her eyes to meet his. "I woke up. I had to bio, of course."

He nods and smiles slightly.

"When my feet touched the floor, I felt tile instead of carpet, and I realized where I was...I looked over and saw you lying there next to me and, well, I guess I just sort of panicked. I meant what I said; I literally didn't know what to do. Because, well, I didn't know what you wanted me to do...what you expected me to do. Not for sure..."

He looks concerned, and furrows his brow slightly, but remains silent.

Her uncomfortable look returns, and that worries Adam. Before he can offer her any sort of reassurance, she resumes talking. "Believe it or not, I haven't really done this kind of thing before." With a somewhat embarrassed look, she plunged onward. "Not really, not quite in this situation, so, like I said, I don't know the rules or the proper etiquette, if you prefer."

She sighs and pulls a cigarette out of her pack and taps the filter end on the arm of the loveseat for a moment before continuing. "I was never into casual sex. Not in high school, college...ever. I never trolled the bars, or was into pickups, or one-night stands. I couldn't do those things because they just held no appeal for me." She shrugged. "It isn't in me. It's not me being prudish. See, for me, there always had to be something there first." Pausing, she looks at him carefully, and says emphatically and yet still softly, "I had to feel something, something deep, for the other person, and more importantly I had to feel that something back from them, too, or I just couldn't do much of anything. I couldn't function. If it wasn't there, it didn't mean anything, and if it didn't mean anything then it wasn't worth doing."

Leaning forward, lifting the cigarette to her lips she slowly lights it. She takes a long pull, and lets the smoke trickle out, and casts her eyes downward, then continues in an even quieter voice. "You and I have been friends a long time, and I have always valued that friendship, more than you realize, probably even now." She raised her eyes to meet his once again. "When I woke up, and saw you there next to me, the first thing I thought of was that now not only will things be different between us, they can't ever be the same again. Thinking that just horrified me. I knew because of what we had done… Well, one way or another, good or bad, it was going to affect our friendship. There's no turning back from what we did, and maybe I'm being selfish, but I didn't want to lose what we had."

Adam knew exactly what she meant by that, but he didn't want to interrupt her. His chance to talk would come soon enough. He waited for her to continue, and as her eyes searched his face, he remained passive and his expression was open.

Nikki went on, watching him, looking for any sign of a negative reaction. "I knew how I felt about what we did, and how I felt about you. But what I didn't know for sure was what you were feeling; I mean, what did this mean to you? What did you want out of…this? Did it mean no more to you than just knocking off a quick piece because I was willing and available, or was there more being offered on the table here?"

He winced a bit at the language but said nothing.

She saw his reaction and wondered if she should have said that, but she had to know. "I had no idea what you'd think about me now, or what you might say to me once you woke up, and if it was bad news, I damn sure didn't want to be sitting in bed naked to hear it. That's why I got dressed and came out here." She shrugged and slipped a stray lock of hair behind her ear. "Neutral territory I suppose."

"You know, it's even more than that," she added, and shaking her head, she said more to herself than to him, "I can't believe I'm going to tell you this, but maybe you'll understand better if I do." She sighs and looks uncomfortable. She looks at him for a long moment. He watches her, patiently waiting.

She takes a breath, and says deliberately and a bit nervously, "You are the third person that I have ever been intimate with. The third. In my forty-nine years, I've slept with three men. Jesus Christ, can you believe that? In both of those situations, we had been in long standing relationships before anything…happened…, and I knew exactly where I stood. You know, the whole courtship ritual song and dance. I suppose the best way I can explain it is, what it comes down to is this; in the morning I knew it was alright to still be there when they woke up."

His ice blue eyes had never wavered from hers the entire time she spoke. She could tell he absorbed each word and every thought she expressed. He had barely moved a muscle the entire time. There had been little reaction to anything she said, especially that last statement, which surprised her. He now appeared to be deep in thought. She let him have all the time he needed. She had nothing else to say now.

Eventually he stood up. Adam picked up his empty coffee cup, and looked over at her cup, then his eyes found hers and he smiled softly. "You know, I bet a lot more people than you think are just like you in that regard. It just never comes up in daily conversation. If it did, I bet you'd be surprised. I'll get you some coffee." She started to get up. "I can get it." He motions to her to stay put. "No, ma'am, nope. That's my job."

He talks as he walks into the kitchen, still talking to her over his shoulder, and liking how her being here made him feel. "If your coffee cup is empty, I'll fill it. If you run out of smokes, even at 3:30 in the morning, I'll run out and get you some." Adam turned and smiled at her through the open doorway. "Although at that hour we should be sleeping and if we were up, we should be doing something else."

Nikki grinned at him, feeling a bit more relaxed with his lighthearted banter. He was talking to her like he always did, and that made her feel better.

"And even if you ran out of those things that only you women use once a month, I'd go run to the store and buy those, too. That's what I should do, that's my job."

She smiles and feels a stab of guilt and shakes her head. She'd heard those same words before, in another life. He sets down her coffee cup on the end table, pauses, smiles a bit and then kisses her on the forehead. Then he walks back to the couch and sits back down. "I don't think what you just told me is all that unusual." Adam said philosophically, "Really, I don't. You should never let how you feel about something be governed by other people's opinions. It's none of their damn business, and who cares what they think about your life's decisions."

He leans forward and puts his elbows on his knees and lights a smoke. Adam inhales deeply, and as he exhales, his eyes narrow a bit. He looks at her for a moment, his cool blue eyes searching hers intently, as though he's weighing if she is truly prepared to hear what he has to say.

Nikki never breaks his gaze, understanding the unspoken

appraisal, and isn't bothered by it in the least. He tilts his head a bit and begins in a conversational way. "What you said made me think. Now, while I can never claim to have had quite the restraint that you possessed in, certain areas, I can say with certainty that there have only been three women in my life that I have ever loved."

Her heart sank like a rock and her mind went into warp drive. "My God", she thought as her heart shrank a size and her mind raced. "Am I really such an idiot that I allowed myself to think he wouldn't screw with my head like he screws with everyone else's? Is what makes this fucker so endearing to me as a friend going to be the same shit that breaks my heart now? Could he take a joke this far? Would he do that to me?" She silently groaned. "He could, but I didn't tell him what I was thinking, did I? So now it's his fault because he didn't read my mind? No, listen to him. He deserves better from me than this. He can only fuck with me if I let him, you stupid bitch.' Considering her last thought, she then corrected herself. 'In fact, isn't that what I just did?'

"The first one," Adam stated evenly, "you already know about, and that was my wife. We were young, and just couldn't keep our hands off each other, and at that stage in my life, I thought that was true love. Every chance we got; we'd be in bed. I thought this was the real deal. After we were married, and real life settled in, I realized that other than being good in bed, we really didn't have a whole lot of other interests in common. We kinda just skipped over all that. It didn't seem important until I came up for air, I suppose. There was no hope of getting her into gaming, so, I tried reverse logic, and tried to get involved in her interests. She didn't seem to appreciate my attempted involvement. I even quit gaming altogether, so I could turn all my attention to what it was that interested her, but she would have none of it. She felt I was intruding into places I had no business being, the things I wasn't involved in, or interested in before...and I just plain wasn't welcome.

"All I was trying to do, was ...be friends...be involved in the daily stuff. I tried explaining that I wanted to share our lives outside the bedroom, but she just didn't buy that. It wasn't her fault actually; her culture dictated that if things were good in bed, and the bills were getting paid, there just was no need for anything more in a marriage...Can you imagine? Nothing else in common was just fine with her and was the norm from her experiences....but not mine. So, I kept trying, but all that did was breed animosity. So much so, in fact, that she began to despise my attempts to get more involved with her interests....and I realized that what made her happy, wasn't nearly enough to make me happy. Well, to make a long story short, eventually I got to the point that I couldn't even stand to be in the same room with her, and for my own sake I just had to end the relationship. And I use that term loosely. Looking back, I can't even call it a relationship because there never truly was one. But at the time, I thought that was love."

He pauses, puts out his smoke, then reaches for another one. She watches, and listens, fascinated not by the story, because she'd heard it before....but fascinated by his openness, and she was wondering where he was going with this train of thought. She knew he was telling her for a reason but knowing him, some of this could be a fabricated fable. But then again, no matter how much he loved to bullshit people, what she saw in his eyes gave her the patience to hear him out even if she still wondered what the hell this had to do with her and the both of them.

Adam smiles at her reassuringly. "Now, the second woman I ever loved, well, that was interesting, to say the least. It was quite a few years later. I had gotten off from work early one Thursday and decided to go have dinner in this steakhouse that I really liked. I usually only felt up to going out for dinner on the weekends; I'd be too beat after work to do much other than grab a shower and play games before I went to bed. That would explain why I never saw this woman before. So, I go in, find a seat at the bar, and across the way on the other side of the bar sits this extraordinarily beautiful woman.

Now, you know me. I just have to go mess with her head, because there isn't a hope in hell she'd be interested in me, so I go sit on the stool next to her and buy her a beer. I figure, what the hell, this will be fun, and all the while I'm looking for her boyfriend that I have no doubt is about to come and pound my ass into oblivion at any moment.

"I get my thoughts in order about what I'm going to lie to her about, when she says to me, "Look, we can sit here and drink a few more beers and waste time, or we can just skip all this bullshit and go to my place and get into bed right now. However," she said, "I have to tell you up front that all that will be involved here is sex. There will be no flowers, no cards, no dates, no commitments and no promises. The only phone call I'll want from you is to see if I'm available when you're in the mood to get laid."

Nikki blinked at him in disbelief, "You have got to be kidding me." she said evenly. "No, not at all." Adam said firmly, "Well, now, I have to admit, I thought that was the most original, and needless to say, bold, pickup line that I had ever heard, especially being used by a woman. I will say that I was somewhat intrigued. I had nothing to lose so, yes, I did indeed go back to her place."

Nikki narrowed her eyes and leaned forward a bit, "Ah, excuse me, I don't wanna hear this shit. Why are you telling me all this?"

He smiled and playfully gave her a wink. "Shush, you. When I get rolling, I can talk up a storm. That's what we're here doing, isn't it? Talking? But you'll see, there's a method to my madness." Adam then looked thoughtful. "Now, where was I? Oh, yeah. So, when things were over, I left."

Nikki laughed when he euphemistically used the word "things", no doubt to spare her delicate sensibilities. Adam noticed, smiling, but continued right along. "It was so, convenient. I just couldn't believe that was all there was going to be required of me. She was beautiful in a way that was exotic, but it was all so superficial, and what she said was so damned unusual that she pulled me right into her game. For her, that's what it was, alright. I wondered why I hadn't seen her before, then I recalled I had never been to that place during the week, and if what she said was true then I'd imagine on the weekends when I would possibly be there she'd be rather, oh…I'd say, fully occupied elsewhere.

"I guess it was my ego, or hormones, or whatever but I thought that I was in love with that woman. At least, I thought that's what it was at the time. I was sure the line she fed me was just to keep her from being disappointed if things didn't work out. I was sure I'd be the one to change her, shall we say, lifestyle. God, what an ass I was…."

Nikki sat stone-faced and didn't grace that remark with a reply.

"I went to work the next day, of course I started asking around about this chick. You know me, I never go out much. And boy, did I get the scoop on her.

Nikki smiled knowingly; the fucker had it coming.

He chuckles ruefully at her expression. "I see that smile of yours, and no, she wasn't a pro, but what she was, was a nymphomaniac."

Nikki's eyes widen, and she tries not to giggle at the look on his face.

"Even better, she knew what she was, and this was how she chose to handle it because, evidently, she liked it!"

Nikki had to laugh at that, even though it seemed he was trying to tell her something, and frankly she wasn't sure she was going to like how this all applied to the two of them.

"So much so, she had been known to see at least 20 different men in any given month. Yeash. And from what I was told, she meant exactly what she had said. No commitments.

"Now, I had to think, what the hell was going on here…they have to be exaggerating; either that, or they didn't pass muster with her and were being vindictive. Yeah, I wish that were the case. So out of curiosity I arranged to see her again."

Nikki muttered under her breath, "Jesus Christ" and shook her head. She'd about had enough of this tale, for whatever purpose it was supposed to serve.

Adam didn't miss her reaction, but he continued without pause. He spoke slowly, driving his point home. "And I have to tell you, it just wasn't the same. Her looks hadn't changed, but knowing what I did, what I thought about the whole thing sure had. I mean, it had been a long time since I had been with anyone, so running into her and having her tell me, well, just come on let's do it was a bit overwhelming. And boy, did I fall for it. So did my ego. But this second time there, I suppose my actual brain was in charge, and to be totally honest, I just couldn't wait until it was over."

Nikki made a scoffing noise and rolled her eyes.

"No, that's the God's honest truth." Adam insisted, "In fact, I kinda had to help it get over, if ya know what I mean, just so I could get outta there and go home." He waved a finger at her and smiled and said with a laugh. "You look amazed, but I'm dead serious."

He puts out his cigarette, then looks back at her and continues in a speculative tone. "Now, maybe if I had met her about 20 years or so earlier, I'd have thought I'd have died and gone to heaven. It's every young man's dream, right? Free sex, no commitments, no effort, just roll up and have at it. No worries. But you know wat That just wasn't what I was looking for; it was easy, but I realized right then and there that wasn't what I wanted, or what I needed."

"Yeah, I see that smirk you're trying to hide." Adam looked closely at Nikki's face, then chuckled a bit, "You're probably gloating inside, thinking I'm a fool for even falling for this nonsense." Then Adam's face grew serious. "But I'm glad it happened, because I came out of that situation having finally learned one of life's biggest lessons. That sex without love, without a relationship, was simply just another means of physical release. Hell, I could do better with my left hand and never have left home. In fact, I have."

Nikki gaped at him, then in spite of her seriousness laughed out loud.

"Now, you must know, I'm telling you all of this for a reason. It all goes back to what you said earlier." He leans forward, then begins speaking, but in a softer, less animated voice. "Earlier, you had said, with those two people you had previously been intimate with, you knew where you stood, and therefore felt comfortable, because you had been in a longstanding relationship with them."

He grins in a slightly bemused, and yet warm way at her.
"Nikki," Adam stated with quiet emphasis, "you and I have known each other
for years. We do, in fact, have a longstanding relationship." He paused and
watched the expression change on Nikki's face as she considered his words.

"It doesn't matter that we actually met each other face to
face for the first time two days ago. It doesn't matter that the first time we
touched was yesterday. What does matter is what we have together. What
we've had all along, as it grew over time. We've spent hours together gaming,
Nikki, four or five hours a night, twelve or more a day on the weekends. You
know me better than anyone alive, and amazingly enough, you still put up
with me.

"You understand me. We understand each other, we may
not agree all the time on a lot of things, but what we are able to do, is agree to
disagree. The point here is that what we have between us is something that
never existed with those other two women I mentioned, and that is a true
relationship. A relationship, a friendship, is the very foundation that must
exist before real love can even hope to have a foothold. At each respective
time, I had strong feelings for those women, and naturally, I called it love. It
was passion, or lust, the excitement of the chase, or even call it a challenge.
But what's obvious to me now, and hopefully to you, is that I called it love
based on what I had experienced in my life up to that point in time. For all I
knew, for me, it was love. But there was so much missing, and I only recently
have had a reason to recognize that.

"Look, let me ask you a question." Adam asked without
pause. "Where are you now?"

"What?" Nikki says with a slight laugh, "Now? Literally?"

Adam replied quickly, urging her to answer. "Yes, right
now…. Don't think about it, just answer the question; where are you,
exactly?"

She looks at him incredulously, then decides, as it usually is
with him, there's a reason for the question, so she plays along and answers it
deadpan and explicitly. "I'm in Denver, Colorado, sitting on a loveseat in your
apartment."

"Uh huh. Bingo. And have you ever heard me say that
anyone has ever been in my apartment? Ok, except the damn cable guy, but
he doesn't count. No, you haven't. I'm surprised at you. You're one of the
ones that give me no end of grief because I won't even order delivery because
I don't want anyone to know where I live, and yet here you are, sitting in what
passes for my living room. Nor, by the way, do I let anyone have my personal
phone number, and, I might point out, you've had my number for years."

Nikki blinked with surprise. This was a lot to take in, and
Adam wasn't finished yet.

"Allow me to elaborate. Those times when I felt the need to experience female company, I always met them at some neutral place or even went to their place, but under no circumstances did I ever bring a woman home. Not even my ex-wife, when she was my fiancée. She even joked that I had a woman tied up in the closet and that's why I wouldn't bring her to my house. I am just a very private person, and I like being that way. Yes, it was partly so I'd never have to worry about being bothered any more than I chose to be by my, we'll call them, brief associations."

Adam looked thoughtfully at her a moment, as if considering saying more. Then he nodded to himself more than to Nikki, and added, "Mostly it had to do with some things I was involved with when I was young and foolish. Back then, keeping where you lived and as much about yourself as possible a secret was pretty much a good idea if you wanted to stay alive."

He looked quickly at Nikki and thought he should clarify that a bit. "I should mention, that was a long, long time ago, and par for the course growing up in the inner city. The only habit I kept as a holdover from those miss-spent days of my youth, was making sure my private life, stayed private. I have to admit; it's served me well for all these years."

Nikki appeared thoughtful, but not disturbed by what he had said. Adam continued, but changing the rhythm of his voice to emphasize his next words. "But the main reason I never brought a woman to my place was that I never wanted my home to become someplace that held bad memories for me. And the last place I ever wanted to be reminded of a broken heart was the bed I slept in every night."

Adam paused, letting that last statement sink in. He leaned forward a bit more, elbows on his knees, his eyes never wavering from hers as he peered at her through the fringe of his jet-black hair. Then he smiled slightly, raised his eyebrows, and waited.

Nikki's eyes widened a bit as the significance of everything he had just implied in his usual beat around the bush method finally began to register. Ok, point made, she was an exception to several of his rules, but what else, what more? Was she just supposed to assume there was more? Yep, there was going to be more, because he got up to refill the coffee cups again.

When Adam came back into the room, this time he set his coffee cup down on the end table by the couch first, and walked over to her, setting her coffee cup down on the end table closest to her. Then he turned and stood in front of her. His eyes found hers again and held them with a gaze that was riveting.

"I'll sum it up with this; do you trust your instincts?"

She blinked and looked slightly taken aback. "Of course, I do."

He grinned warmly. "One of the distinctive qualities about yourself that you mentioned a while ago was this; you said not only did you have to feel something deep for the person you were with, but you also had to feel that same something deep back from them, or you just couldn't function." Lowering his voice, Adam then asked her directly, "Do you have any reason at all to believe that this has somehow changed for you? That this reciprocal feeling no longer has to be there? Because," he added, allowing a small amount of amusement to show, "as I recall last night, there was quite a bit of "functioning" going on."

Nikki smiled at him and slowly answered, "No, of course that hasn't changed for me, but Adam, this is you we're talking about."

Adam shook his head. "No, it's us we're talking about here, Nikki. So what does your gut tell you? I'll ask you again; do you trust your instincts?"

"Yes." she restated softly, then more emphatically. "Yes, I do."

Adam nodded. "And that brings us to the third woman I ever loved." His smile broadened and reached out his hand to her. Nikki gave him her hand, he then held it and he gently pulled her up to him.

When she stood, he kissed her on the forehead, then her cheek, then took her in his arms and held her close. Then Adam relaxed his embrace and ran his fingers up the sides of her arms, over her shoulders, until his hands lightly held her face. He looked into her eyes, and then gave her a soft, gentle, lingering kiss on the lips. Then he guided her back to the loveseat. He slid his hands back down her arms, and said softly, "Have a seat, this may take a while."

She sat on the end of the loveseat where she had been sitting, and he sat on the other end. He turned in the chair with his back to the armrest so he could see her, and she did the same. Adam took a deep breath, and with a wry smile he began. "Those two women I talked about before, I suppose I did love them. At least what I thought love was, at those times. I suppose it was the type of love I was capable of at the time that I knew each of them….it was all I could feel, and all I knew how to feel, then. I know now that the love I had experienced back then was shallow and baseless. I thought it was the real thing, but it now it's clear what I felt was so superficial. I didn't know that then, but I sure as hell know it now.

"I guess it's because I never let anyone really know the real me, to get that close to me. It's just how I am. You're the only one to really experience the real me, and not go running away, screaming. The time you and I spent gaming and talking…we ended up knowing each other pretty darn well over time. We became friends. And of course, it's natural to make friends ingame when you play as much as we do, and God knows we have a lot of them, but this was different. You, you were able to get past my shell, and more amazingly to me, I let you do it. That must tell you something. You were able to read me like a book. I always enjoyed talking to you, because you're almost as smart as I am."

"Hey!" she said indignantly as she swats at his arm, and he laughs softly at her chagrin. He deftly catches her hand, and then holds it. Then he looks at her hand, then slowly looks up to her face, and his expression becomes quietly intent. "But, now, I know there's so much more to love, so much more that has to be there; a foundation. If you're lucky, a friendship first, then if you're really fortunate, a relationship grows from that."

He lifts her hand to his lips, and softly kisses her fingers, then holds her hand gently in both of his hands. Then his eyes travel slowly back up from her hand to her face and his ice blue eyes stare into hers. "The third woman that I have ever loved is in my apartment, sitting on my loveseat, right here in front of me."

Nikki slowly smiles as she sees in his expression how serious he is, and tilts her head downward, looking at the hand he is still holding. She places her other hand on top of his, and then peers at his face.

With his right hand he lightly strokes her hair, then traces the outline of her cheek until he reaches her chin. Leaning forward slowly, Adam kisses her again, softly, and lingeringly.

When their lips part Adam's eyes search her face for any sign of disapproval. Seeing none, he asks her quietly, "Honestly, that doesn't surprise you, does it? Yes, God help me, I admit it, I love you. I said before, that everything I've told you tonight was for a reason. I wanted you to understand me, and where I was coming from. I wanted you to know that I was sincere. I knew you meant a great deal to me, but I didn't know just how much until yesterday."

"Yesterday?" Nikki considered that carefully. "Humm, and what was it that happened yesterday?" Then her eyes flashed a warning. "And if you say it's because we ended up in bed, I'm going to be very disappointed."

Adam's expression became thoughtful. "Technically, that was today. But yesterday? Well, several things of note happened. In addition, a while after you got here, something started eating at me, and I just couldn't put my finger on it. Last night I managed to figure out exactly what it was, then I was able to come to grips with it."

"That sounds a bit ominous." Nikki intoned, "Can you tell me? Or would I rather not know?"

Adam chuckled self-consciously. "It wasn't anything that you did that I had to deal with, but it was about you, after a fashion. Let's just say that yesterday I resolved a few things that I was wrestling with, all of which has to do with my own stubbornness and self-absorption. My own contrariness got in the way of me seeing the obvious."

"What the hell are you talking about now?" Nikki grinned and waited for his answer.

He looked at her and shrugged helplessly, "I'm trying to tell you, but for this to make sense, I'm going to have to start at the beginning. From when, when I started to notice things; you're kinda asking me to start in the middle here."

Nikki looked slightly puzzled, then she smirked. "And this is new, how?"

Adam grinned back at her and bit his bottom lip so Nikki knew he was refraining from making a smart assed remark. She chuckled quietly and to Adam her gentle laugh was comforting.

Nikki's face brightened as she considered something. Adam was beginning to recognize that look. It meant a question was coming. "Let me ask you something." she said slowly.

"Oh boy, here it comes" Adam muttered, putting on a look of feigned steadfastness.

"I wonder," Nikki haltingly asked, softly, always watching his eyes. "I wonder; just when did you know your feelings for me, had changed?"

Breaking into an admiring grin, Adam almost giggled with delight. "Oh, clever girl! That's not a question that has a one word, or one sentence, or certain time, or an exact place, kind of an answer, now is it?" He appeared to consider what to say next, and once satisfied, he smiled and gave her hand a squeeze. "It was more like over a period of time, and certain things happened at one time or another since you've been here that made me acutely aware that I cared far more about you than I had realized."

Nikki countered his seriousness with some gentle teasing. "Well, we are talking about you here, aren't we? Nothing that involves you is ever simple. You're complex as hell, and you're proud of it! You over analyze everything, and you think for one moment that I'd expect a simple answer from you?"

Adam's face became expressionless and he answered in a monotone, "No." As he looks at her, he attempts to assume an innocent face, while he arches an eyebrow and smiles. They both dissolve into laughter. "In my defense we're not talking about just me, here. It's complex, dang it. More than you might realize. We're talking about you and me. What having you here did to me; did for me. I'll try to explain all that, but I'm

30

gonna have to make more coffee for this one."

As Adam walks toward the kitchen, Nikki watches him go, and the clock catches her eye. "Ah, Adam? I'd really love to hear this now, in fact I don't know if I can possibly stand it if I don't, but it is 5am. I hate to be the one to say this, but don't you have to get ready for work?"

He looked at the clock on the coffeemaker and grunted. "Ugh. So it is. Damn. We've been talking for an hour and a half?"

Nikki smiled indulgently and tried not to stare at Adam as he stood framed in the doorway. "Yes, you have, anyway."

He gives her a look of mild frustration. "That's just it; if I had talked more to the point last night, you'd have woken up in a much better mood. Not too much better, from what I've seen…but enough."

She smiles, stands up and stretches, "Sorry, I'm not, and never have been, a morning person."

Walking into the kitchen, Nikki passes close to Adam and lets her hip graze his as she passes. Adam shakes his head and grins after appreciatively watching her stretch, and as she brushes against him he groans inwardly with a different type of appreciation. Looking at the clock he groans aloud. "Dammit." He looks at Nikki sadly then sighs and shrugs. "Oh well. When do you have to be at your meeting?"

"I don't." she said simply.

"Huh?" Adam remarked in surprise, stopping in his tracks. "Say again?" He turns to look at her quizzically not sure he can believe his ears.

"My meeting ended yesterday. Today and Friday are vacation days."

Motionless, he stares at her "Really." After another second or so, Adam moves toward the living room. "Excuse me for just a moment." Quickly striding out of the kitchen to the living room, Adam picks up his cell phone and begins to dial.

Nikki watches him for a second, then finishes making the coffee, not sure what to do next. She walks to the window and looks outside, trying not to listen to his conversation.

"Hello, Steven? Hey, man, it's Adam. How ya been? That baby sleeping through the night yet?" Adam listens for a moment. "Well, good, glad to hear it, but I bet you're even happier. Yeah, once they get a little size on them, and they can sleep through the night. It makes it so much easier. Well, at least you and Blanche can be on the same shift now. Who me? I'm doing great, man, in fact," glancing at Nikki, he grins sheepishly at her. "I'm better than ever. To tell you the truth, that's why I called. I need to take a couple of personal days; I'll be back in the office on Monday. If folks need me, I'm just a phone call away, but I don't think there's anything they need to finish up this week that they can't handle without me."

Nikki's jaw drops, then she snaps it shut as Adam silently chuckles at her reaction.

Adam listens to Steven for a moment more. "No, nothing's wrong. Everything's fine. Steven, the thing is, I have a friend in town visiting, and she leaves on Sunday."

He abruptly stops talking, blinks, and looks surprised, "Well, yes, yes she is...she does. Steven, how the hell? Oh, no shit? I didn't know Blanche knew Evelyn. Every Wednesday night, huh? Well, I'll be damned." He listens for a moment, then looks at Nikki and shakes his head, grinning wryly.

"You were? Steven, that's damn generous of you. No, but I appreciate it, even though it didn't come to that. Yeah, yeah, yeah. Well, you know where to find me if you need me. Listen, thank you. I owe you. Really. Ok, and thanks again. Bye."

He sets down his cell phone. "Oh," Adam said with a rueful smile and a shake of his head. "I am so busted."

She looks at him with mild curiosity and walking over to him, hands him his coffee. "How so?"

Adam gives her a quick kiss, and she sits on the couch. He follows her and sits next to her. "Well, you heard my side of it."

Nikki looks at him apologetically, "I tried not to listen."

He shrugs and looks a bit sheepish. "Impossible not to overhear in this place, don't worry about it. Anyway, that was Steven Goldman; he's a senior partner of my company. He's the closest thing I have to an immediate supervisor. When you said your meeting was over, well, let's put it this way, I have leave to burn. Anyway, when I said I had a friend visiting, he tells me, "Oh yes, quite a lovely friend, too. Beautiful auburn hair, amazing blue eyes? You two make a nice couple." Shocked the hell outta me."

Nikki blinked in surprise. "How'd he know?"

"Of course, you remember Evelyn, the older lady we met at the festival last night?"

Nikki nodded and began to smile.

"Turns out she and Steven's wife play bingo every Wednesday night at the same church. It seems that Evelyn not only gave Blanche the whole low down on us, but also the little minx apparently took pictures of us with her cell phone camera. She showed them to Blanche, and emailed them to her, too."

Nikki's hand goes to her mouth in surprise, and she laughs sympathetically at poor Adam's look of discomfort. "Oh," she chuckles. "That's too funny."

"Yeah," Adam resumes with a touch of sarcasm, "Steven said Blanche came home last night and couldn't wait to get in the door to tell him everything Evelyn had told her. And," Adam dryly reported, "according to Steven, the content of those pictures totally negates my contention at the time that you and I were just friends."

"Uh oh, just what did she take pictures of?"

He grins sheepishly. "I'm...not exactly sure."

"Well, now I definitely want to see those pictures," Nikki chuckled softly.

"You and me, both. Steven said he'd send them to me. He also said," Adam's face took on a bemused look, "That if he hadn't heard from me by noon today, he was going to call me and tell me to take the rest of the week off."

"That's amazingly generous. He seems like a nice guy."

Adam nodded thoughtfully. He always knew Steven was good people, but this would have been beyond anything he would have expected. "So, between the pictures themselves, and what Blanche must have told him, relayed from Evelyn," Adam shrugged. "I just hope I see those pictures before Evelyn decides to post them up on the break room bulletin board."

"And is that so bad?" Nikki asked him without sympathy, "There's nothing wrong with your employees knowing that you're human." He looks at her in surprise, and Adam's tone got defensive but there was laughter in his eyes. "Yes, there is! Now they'll have dirt on me. They'll be talking about this for years!"

She rolls her eyes and reached for a smoke. "Oh, for Christ's sake, quit whining."

"I'm joking," he clarifies. "Sorta."

"Look at it this way," she offered with a playful wink "Think of it as a management relations tool. It'll give them something to talk with you about that isn't work related. Kind of a team building exercise."

He looks at her incredulously. "You're killing me here. The last thing I want to talk to them about is my personal life."

She shrugs, unfazed. "Well, at least now they know you have one."

His eyes twinkle in contrast to his vehement response. "I'll deny it to my death."

Nikki's face falls, and Adam realizes what he's inadvertently said. "Oh Nikki, I'm sorry... I didn't mean..."

Nikki reaches out and squeezes his hand. "It's ok. I know you didn't..." She sighs and says with resignation, "Ok, look, just take their teasing in the spirit it is given. They talk about you every day; you just never hear it. People just do that about the boss. You were talking to Evelyn last night for a while, more than you were required, to just be courteous. And, really, do you think she'd post anything like that knowing how you'd react to it? In fact, knowing you, the poor woman may be scared to death about it."

"Evelyn? Oh no, she's not scared of me one bit. In fact, the reason why we talked for so long was she was trying to convince me that you and I just had to be more than friends, and if we were, if I didn't do something to change that, then I was clearly an idiot."

Nikki looked amused. "That nice lady actually called you an idiot?"

"Yes, indeed, she did," Adam confirms, and then his voice softens, and he looks at Nikki affectionately, "And it's a damn good thing for her that I had been thinking the same thing all day myself."

Nikki blinks at him, and now it was her turn to look thoughtful. "You did, huh?" and reaches for her cigarettes, then she says, "I wonder what it was that made her say that."

"I guess she saw things objectively. She's a sharp old lady, that one. Kind of a Hispanic yenta. She said she had been watching the two of us together ever since she caught sight of us leaving the restaurant." Adam features took on an amused expression. "She said we had "lover" written all over us."

She laughs softly at the way Adam said that and thought that it was interesting that neither one of them had seen it so clearly. But then, they both had things to sort through before daring to venture out loud what either one of them had been mulling over.

Responding to the look of contemplation on Nikki's face, Adam offered, "But, see, she wasn't inside my head, so she didn't know about all the things I was wrestling with."

"What things? Adam? You said that before, and I gotta wonder just what the hell you're talking about."

"Well, that's what I was going to tell you about before you mentioned what time it was, and then dropped that pleasant surprise on me that you have two whole days here that weren't going to be tied up with being at a conference. I didn't expect that. Now that I don't have to go to work, and you don't have to be anywhere, we have plenty of time for me to tell you about that."

He reaches for her free hand, picks it up, and lightly kisses her fingers. With a wicked grin, his voice took on a mischievous tone. "Think I'll get some more coffee, want some?"

Nikki looks at Adam with affection and exasperation. "Adam!" she hisses through her teeth. "You Goddamn tease, you better tell me!"

Adam instantly acquires a look of exaggerated innocence and patience. "You asked me when I knew how I felt about you had changed. No, I didn't forget. I never forget anything. Well, the answer to that question also holds the answer about what I was wrestling with..." He smiles and winks, as he walks to the kitchen, much to Nikki's exasperation. He says over his shoulder, "It'll make sense eventually, and you'll understand exactly what all my cryptic comments meant, I promise." Nikki thinks to herself in mild consternation that he had damn well better hope so.

Adam comes back into the living room, talking as he walks toward the couch, then stands in front of her as he began his tale. "When I decided I was going to surprise you at the airport, I had no preconceived notion of any of this happening, no nefarious scheme, nothing of the sort. I was just damn glad to finally be able to meet you." Adam looked at her and nodded for emphasis, and she had no difficulty believing him, since she had no idea this would happen, either. "When you told me, you had to travel out here for that conference, and asked if I'd be interested in meeting for dinner, well of course I said yes. I thought it'd be a blast. I'd show you around a bit, play the host, and we'd have some fun with the unsuspecting locals. Then I got to thinking, there can't be that many flights arriving here on that day from your neck of the woods, so I started doing some research." His face took on sort of a guilty smile. "I knew you'd never get up early enough for the earliest morning arrivals, and I hoped to God you had the sense not to arrive alone and in a strange town as late as 11pm." Adam glanced at her as though he still wasn't sure about her level of common sense, and Nikki made a quick face at him. "I thought it was a safe bet that you'd arrive on one of the midday flights. They arrived a few hours apart," he shrugged "but, I figured, screw it; I'll give it a shot. I work close enough to the airport, so it wouldn't be a huge pain in the ass to try to pull this off. Odds are you'd call me when you got into town. If I managed to miss you when you arrived at the airport, I'd be able to get wherever you were pretty damn quick."

She smiled and toyed with her lighter. He never rambled on for no reason...this was story hour. Well, she'd asked a question, and by God, it looks like he was going to answer every nuance of it before he was done.

"Oh," Adam noticed he was still holding her coffee cup and was still standing. "Guess I could sit, huh?" Grinning sheepishly, he set her refilled coffee cup back down and sat next to her. Nikki realized he was absorbed in telling her his story, so she just grinned at him and didn't harass him about forgetting to sit. Adam flashed a grateful and amused smile her way as he got comfortable. He took a sip of his black coffee, set his cup back down and continued.

"So, the day you arrived, by 3 o'clock I was heading out the door, yelling that if anyone needed me, I had the cell on. I got to the airport and parked. Oh my God, who knew so many people used that damn place during the week?"

She smiled inside at his complaining. It was so, so him.

"I parked, went inside, and straight downstairs to the Baggage Claim in case you beat me there...no one down there bore even the slightest resemblance to you. I scanned the taxi stand, no one there like you. I went up the escalator and had to wait just at the top. No ticket, no entry...damn security. Anyway, soon, I thought I saw someone that might be you," and his face got that familiar teasing look again, "and yup, sure enough, that person headed straight for the ladies room, so I knew it had to be you."

She squeaks in amusement and a bit of irritation and throws a couch pillow at him, and then laughs as he catches it, and hands it back to her.

Adam doesn't lose his momentum at all and continues to recount his recollection of that day. "Now, as I'm waiting it strikes me that I wanted to surprise you, yes, but not scare the hell out of you." His face looks positively impish. "Not that if it happened, it wouldn't be fun as hell, but there's folks with guns walking around that might not be too happy with me if you screamed or something girlie like that." Nikki looks slightly offended. "Scream? I never scream." "Well, I wouldn't say, scream, exactly," Adam mused, "but something similar." She ponders that, and he gets an amused look on his face, and points with his eyes toward the bedroom door. Adam brings his eyes back to Nikki, and she blushes furiously, muttering "...asshole..." under her breath.

He makes a wry smile knowing she's being playfully annoyed and not really as pissed as she sounded. He continued with his monologue, but in the back of his mind still savoring his most recent memories of last evening. "I knew I couldn't run up and grab you and hug you. Besides the possibility of getting shot, you might just knock my lights out. I figured you might not recognize me right away if you saw me, but I knew for damn sure the one thing you would recognize would be my voice." She smiled tenderly in acknowledgement. "You're right about that."

"When you came out of the Ladies Room, finally, and headed toward Baggage Claim I started to follow you. Like any red-blooded male, I noticed the view, and God help me, I enjoyed it." His gaze moved to her legs pulled up next to her on the couch, and back to her face. He shook his head a bit and a smile of delight tried to make an appearance. Then he became more serious. "It's not that I'm such a letch, I just didn't know you had such damn good-looking legs, among other things. I was enjoying it so much that we were almost to the escalators before I remembered you still didn't know I was there."

"I had been pondering what I should to say to you, but I finally decided to keep it simple, so I went with something familiar. "My God, I thought you'd never get outta that bathroom." Adam's eyes twinkled as he chuckled. "Man, I never saw anyone stop so dead in their tracks. That slow turn around you made was classic." Nikki laughed and patted his thigh, "Oh, you got me good, alright. I couldn't believe what I had heard, let alone that you were there. I couldn't believe it!"

Adam's face then took on a look of annoyance. "Neither could I when you told me what hotel you were staying at. Good lord, there's stories in the paper every day about the vandalism, muggings and even rapes that happen in that district. I couldn't believe they sent a woman to that place." Nikki shrugged. "Don't worry, I'll mention that to the travel agency."

He shook his head in disbelief, but then he became amused. "So I asked where your meeting was going to be, and since I lived eight blocks from there, I suggested you stay at my place. I made a perfectly logical argument. I'd be safer, cheaper, and I could also keep an eye on you better and keep you out of trouble." He laughed softly and looked at her in wonder and with mock accusation. "And you said, 'Ok.' Seemed like the most natural thing in the world for me to do, right?" Nikki nodded, because it did just flow out of him at the time. "Yeah well, it sure came out that way. But what you didn't know then, but do now, is as soon as I said it, I had broken rule numero uno." Adam then intoned mysteriously, "Nobody can know where I live." They both laugh, then Adam smiles slightly and looks thoughtful.

"Now, I knew what I had done, and I had honestly surprised the hell out of myself. No one made me do it, you surely didn't suggest it. I didn't think twice about it, it just seemed the right thing to do given the situation. But I assure you, I have never asked anyone to stay at my place before, especially not a woman. But with you, it just came out like naturally it was not only the right thing to do; it was the only thing to do. Now, if you had protested, or insisted that you'd stay in a hotel, I'd have gone along with it to a point, but I'd have been such a pain in the ass being so picky and protective that you'd have caved just to shut me up! By the way, I'm still surprised that you said yes, but that's neither here nor there."

Nikki had surprised herself with that answer, too. It was interesting that Adam seemed to have been sharing the same thoughts that she had been mulling at that stage of the evening. Truth be told, if pressed, she couldn't tell him why she said yes, either, other than the simple fact that it just felt right. That it was ok to say yes. She grinned a bit and gave her attention back to Adam. He noticed she'd been introspective and nodded before he began speaking again. "I thought about that the whole way back to my place, I kept asking myself, 'Now, why on earth did you do that?' I kept waiting to feel like I had made some horrible mistake, but I didn't feel that way at all. The thing was, I couldn't figure out why I didn't feel that way. Obviously, it had to be because it was you. But then, why was that? Ok, it's because we were friends and as such, neutral ground, yeah, that had to be it. Was it, though? Around and around that question just buzzed through my head." "I couldn't tell," Nikki helped him out some, "you were doing such a good job as a tour guide."

He inclined his head and smiled. "Thank you. So. We arrive here, and I bring you up to the 'inner sanctum'. Instead of fussing with your makeup, and nosing around the apartment, all the things I expected you to do, you just dropped your bags by the door and said, "Nice place; but I'm hungry". Naturally, my response was, "Well, let's go out and find a place to eat." I thought that steakhouse would be a good place; and no, it's not –that-steakhouse," he replied quickly as Nikki gained a look of recognition. Adam was satisfied she accepted that, even if she did give him a look, and he added "Good service, nice menu, reasonable prices, and in a nice part of town."

Adam stopped, and he looked at Nikki with tenderness and a bit of surprise in his eyes. "Nikki, I never had so much fun having dinner. The food was good, but the conversation was better, much better, than the food could ever hope to be. I think we talked about wallpapering, of all things, for a good thirty minutes. We talked about any and everything, because with you, it was so easy. The best thing about it was, you just were so… yourself. It was so apparent you didn't feel the need to impress me, but you damn sure weren't going to let me get away with anything, either. You knew when to call me on my bullshit, and I found that refreshing, and amusing, and…endearing. I started to notice little things here and there. Things like, your eyes were such a lovely shade of blue, how long your lashes were, how absolutely perfect your nails were polished, even down to your littlest toenails, which reminds me about those legs of yours again. How your hair was such a wonderful color…and how it shined and almost glimmered as it caught the candlelight." Nikki squirmed a bit as the compliments rained down around her.

Adam smiled indulgently but made no comment on her apparent discomfort. He figured she'd just have to get used to hearing it, because he didn't ever intend to stop telling her how she captivated him so completely. "As we talked, I noticed at one time or another, some of the folks in the place would look at you, or us, and smile. At first I wondered about that. We weren't being loud or obnoxious. Then maybe it was because you were new in town. Eventually I figured they just enjoyed seeing some people actually being genuinely happy and enjoying themselves. Later on it occurred to me that could be because we looked like 'the happy couple', you know? Well, I thought, the jokes on them, we weren't a couple." He paused and continued with a bit of surprise in his voice, "The second I thought that, I was hit with this overwhelming sadness….and I asked myself, what the hell was that all about? I chalked it up to being tired…and let it go. Temporarily, anyway."

He noticed Nikki was paying attention to his every word, and Adam realized he could very easily get accustomed to times this tender on a regular basis. For the first time since he could remember Adam felt warm and content, and he wanted this moment to go on forever. Smiling warmly, he ran a finger down her wrist and softly told her more of the story. "After you had about three jaw cracking yawns in a row, I decided we'd better get back. Low and behold, we'd been sitting there about four hours; sure didn't seem like it, you were surprised too. You said that happens every time we talk, so how could I be surprised. I asked you what you meant, and you said "Once we start talking….we just seem to talk until something makes us stop." You know, I thought about that, and damned if that wasn't the case. Thing is, I never thought about it that way before.

"When we get back here, I tell you that you can have the bed, and I'll sleep on the couch. You said that was fine, but…. But something inside me felt like it was all wrong. I actually stopped and thought about that; I figured it was the whole "rule numero uno" thing, and how you being here was such a blatant transgression of my own self enforced order. When you were brushing your teeth and I was getting the extra linens out, my thoughts came back to this. Just what was bothering me? I was delighted you were here, wasn't I? So that wasn't it. Or was it? I sat down on the couch and thought about that. Maybe that was it, was I too happy that you were here? Now, I know that sounds a bit ridiculous. But the more I thought about it, the more it felt like I had just been on a terrific date, not a night out with a friend.

Adam gave Nikki a slightly self-conscious look, "I thought to myself, "But, what's wrong with that?" The answer was there, it just kept eluding me. And you know, even though I couldn't put my finger on it, I just knew ...something just kept... gnawing at me. The closest I can describe the feeling is that it's like when you walk into a room and forget why you went in there in the first place."

"About then you came back into the living room and asked if I'd mind if you caught the news on TV before you went to bed. Of course, I didn't mind. Do you remember how you were sitting, like you are now, with your legs tucked up next to you on the couch? As we sat there, making conversation about the news, I actually caught myself about to reach over and caress your leg. Now, the sheer terror of wondering if you saw that or not, told me I had some serious thinking to do. I mean, it's not like I was trying to make a pass at you or anything as gauche as that. It was more like...just something I should be doing at that time...in that situation....an act of familiarity, of intimacy....it felt so right, so natural that I almost actually did it without consciously being aware of doing it. Nikki raised her eyebrows slightly, but as far as Adam could tell, she didn't act like she had noticed that little maneuver. Even though he was telling her about it now, he was still relieved that his error went unnoticed.

"The news ended, and you said you were beat and had to go to bed. In a way, I was relieved, because I had to figure out just what the hell was going on with me. You gave me a hug, and a kiss on the cheek, and said thank you for dinner; that you had a wonderful time. I so wanted to give you a kiss back, just a peck on the cheek, but I couldn't do it. Mind you, not that I didn't want to do it, I damn sure did. I just could not do it. I asked again what time you needed to be up, and 5am worked for you, so getting up and out the door at the same time was not going to be a problem. You went into the bedroom and closed the door, and the light went out. Now I was all alone with my thoughts, and my dilemma."

"I turned out the lights and stretched out on the couch. There was thunderstorm off in the distance, I could see the lightening, but couldn't yet hear the thunder. It looked like it was a pretty active storm, and that made me wonder if you were frightened by storms. Then I remembered you had once asked me if I thought thunderstorms were romantic." He smiled at the memory, and then turned that smile towards Nikki. "I never had given the matter any thought before you had asked me, and found that if I considered it, yes, sometimes, they were. It occurred to me that no one else had ever asked me anything like that before. And how that was so like you; making me think about ordinary things in extraordinary ways."

Adam grinned then shrugged, giving her a little wink. "Then

again, no one else had ever been invited to spend the night here before, let alone made me sleep on the couch, and somehow, I didn't mind it one bit. Why the hell was that?" Nikki shook her head in reply, but she knew he already knew the answer.

"As the storm crept closer, I was still wide awake. Not because of the storm, but because I was still thinking about you. I was remembering how great a time I had, and how much fun it was to spend time with you. I tried to stop thinking about you, and to get some sleep, but try as I might, my thoughts would come right back to you....I knew you were right there in the next room, I could practically hear you breathing. I caught myself wishing we could have another evening together tomorrow night. Then I thought that would be pushing my luck. Pushing my luck? What the hell was that all about? What's going on here...it's not like we're dating. No, but, that's what it felt like to me. I wanted it to be like that. Then I wondered, could that be it? Am I falling in love with Nikki?" My instant reaction to that was, "Naw, come on, man, you can't... "

"But, dammit, why not? Holy shit, was that what this was all about? Maybe...yup, had to be. There it is. I realized this was exactly what kept happening all evening long. It's like I had this internal argument going on at a subconscious level. Every time I'd think of you, in any way of appreciation....of how pretty you were, how wonderful it was to see you when I talked to you, it was as though this wall would slam down and stop my train of thought. Like, somehow it was wrong for me to think of you in that way." Adam nodded sagely and Nikki laughed at his offbeat way of recounting their evening. She had been sorting out her own feelings about the last few days, but none of that mattered until she heard what Adam had to say. She was enjoying this as much as he was, so she smiled encouragingly to him. After a sip of coffee, he leaned forward, giving her a quick kiss, then he grinned and continued.

"Ok, now I was getting somewhere...I knew the "what", the trick was going to be to figure out the "why". The storm was almost here but was fading as it drew nearer. It made me think it wanted to try to stealth by, but still makes its presence known. Strong when it needed to be, but capable of being gentle when it wanted to be. I smiled, because I once made that analogy about myself to you one night; strong enough to be gentle."

"Gentle, me? Gentle?" Adam laughed heartily. "The very idea, thinking of me as gentle cracks me up. I thought about how many times in game I had to check my temper or impatience with people who were being just plain stupid. It amused me thinking about some classic moments in game

41

when people had just lost it. About how funny it was when it was someone else making an ass out of themselves for once, instead of me." Nikki gave him dubious look, but Adam waved it off and went on, "I took comfort in the fact that just about everyone I knew at one time or another had lost their temper while playing...you included, but then I thought of one person who never did.... Well, I sat bolt upright on the couch. It all just came together so fast; all the pieces of the puzzle just clicked into place." Adam looked at Nikki and slowly his face became introspective. "Now I knew exactly what it was that was eating me all day long."

Adam takes both her hands in his, sighs and gave her a here goes nothing look, and says ruefully, "What I had been doing apparently, was still thinking of you as...being married." Nikki looked sharply at Adam, more than a bit taken aback, and started to pull back her hands from his grasp, but he wouldn't release them. "Now wait. Hear me out. You need to know, I'm not going to tell you this because I want to stir up what must be terribly painful memories for you. I'm telling you because ...It's because that fact had been burned into my subconscious so deeply, that, well, I could only allow myself to... Nikki, my feelings; I was used to only allowing them to go so far." His eyes held a look of appeal, hoping she'd understand his honest and accurate assessment of what he had been feeling and thinking. Nikki still looked at him darkly. No doubt she understood what he said, but it was clear to him she didn't quite make the mental connection that he had made.

Adam takes a deep breath and slowly let it out. "Let me try to explain this better. When we first met, you were married to Michael. And all of the years I have known you, you were married to Michael."

Nikki looks at Adam reproachfully and he can feel her physically tense with discomfort. But Adam gently, and hopefully reassuringly, squeezes her hands. "Nikki, you've got to hear me out about this. It's as difficult for you to hear, as it is for me to say it."

Nikki takes Adam at his word, and listens, but still eyes him cautiously.

Adam sighs a bit and goes on; he has to try to make her understand. "As I got to know you, I considered you a friend, but also, I knew, on every level, you were Michael's wife. That's just how it was and part of the package. I was ok with that, of course I was. It was...a large part of who you were, and so that's how I thought of you, I guess you could say, how I categorized you. And as such, of course, you were totally off limits; it never occur to me to ever allow myself to even begin to think of another man's wife as anything more than a friend. A damn good friend, at that, but...that's as far as it went; as far as I'd allow it to go...because if I did or said something stupid…I would risk losing what I did have, and that was our friendship. A no brainer if ever there was one."

"I was so used to thinking of you in that context. I never really had a reason to allow myself to think of you in any other light…until yesterday. Before then, in all of our playing, joking and teasing with each other; there was a line we never crossed. That's how it should have been, and so that's how it was." He pauses, and his expression changes to one more somber. Looking down for a moment, trying to find a way to put into words what he needed to say next, Adam finally looks up, and very quietly says, "When you told me about the accident…God, I felt like I… Nikki, I don't think I can really describe it. I was devastated on two fronts, the shock of losing Michael, and just imagining what you must be going through…"

She looks down abruptly, then away, and sighs heavily, "If you have a point, please, make it and move on."

He nods his head, then gazes out the window for a moment. He squeezes her hands gently, and then begins again. "I could tell a lot about him simply by how he chose to behave. I really can't say we were more than acquaintances, but I truly respected Michael, and, well I guess because of that, I also respected how he must have felt about you. He must have been a wonderful man, if someone like you loved him. I always thought he was a lucky man to have you; then again, a lot of us thought that way."

"That's why I couldn't see the forest for the trees, so to speak. I always have cared about you, but never could afford to even entertain the idea that maybe what I felt about you…in a different time, or place, might become much more than just caring, if given the chance. There just was no reason to think that way. And now, we find ourselves here, you and I. We are in that different place, and at that different time in our lives. A circumstance that we never presumed would happen, but somehow it did. I wasn't planning on any of this to happen when you came here, and I don't think you were either." Nikki gave him a quivering smile, and seeing it almost undid him. "I never intended…."

Adam shook his head, interrupting her before she said something he didn't want to hear. "You have to understand this, though, Nikki. People we love, they become a part of us that we never lose. I know, in certain ways, Michael will always be with you. It's only natural. I must have been aware of that, deep down inside, and so it somehow still felt wrong to feel so strongly about you."

Nikki had been avoiding eye contact with Adam; hearing this was hard enough, but she could hear in his voice that he was being honest about what he thought. Still, having Adam of all people, reminded her of Michael, and right now, wasn't helping her feel as good as she thought she did about this whole thing. It was for the same reasons, that Adam had his misgivings. Fair enough, then.

Adam's voice became somewhat pensive as he watched the emotions play across Nikki's face. This was for the best, he thought with certainty. Get it out in the open and see what happens next. He was pouring his honesty out for both of them to examine. He decided to go on, while Nikki was still listening. "You know, as I was examining all this in my head and I finally figured I had come to grips with what was eating at me, right about then, I heard a long, lingering rumble of thunder." Adam looked at Nikki with a bit of amazement. "I actually got a chill up my spine It felt like he was up there, watching me. It was as if he was warning me, not away from you, but to be there for you."

Nikki gasped quietly and looked quickly down, then she stared at the wall, she had to look anywhere but at Adam. She already had been battling with her own feelings. She felt guilty for enjoying herself while she was here. Guilty that she was feeling things again that made her happy. The worst guilt of all was knowing she was beginning to feel this kind of love again, but for someone other than Michael. Never did she think that was going to be possible. She was certain that part of her died that day with Michael, and Nikki had firmly held no thought or even desire of her heart's resurrection.

A.F.K.

CHAPTER III

Unbidden and unwanted, her thoughts leapt back to the old man in the cemetery, and his parting words to her. For a moment, she felt disjointed from the reality of where she was as her mind recalled the cemetery several days ago. She could almost feel the bitterly cold granite headstone on her fingertips when she longingly and lovingly touched it in parting. The memory seemed to be transparent in appearance now; still there and very real but seeming to pull away from her on its own volition. Here and now, someone dear to her had just told her that he loved her, while her hands felt the warmth of his touch as he held her hands in his. She cast her eyes downward again, trying to hide the fact that guilt and happiness both fought for her at that moment. She bites her lower lip, but a tear slipped out anyway, silently, slowly down her cheeks.

Adam had been watching the emotions play across Nikki's face and felt a pang of guilt for the honesty he had to deliver. He saw her struggle and intended to let her find her balance, but then he caught sight of the stray tear sliding down her cheek that she seemed to ignore. Adam couldn't ignore it, however. "Oh…now see what I've done. Dammit, I am so sorry, Nikki…." She looked embarrassed and tried to shrug off her feelings. "It's ok, I just get like this sometimes…I…I can't help it. It creeps up on me." More like it just hit you right between the eyes, Adam thought. But there was no need to state the obvious. He knew she was just trying to deflect the blame for her being upset away from him and back on her. How so very much like her. Adam fervently swore to himself; he didn't want to cause her discomfort but there was no way to avoid it and still be honest with her.

He snags a few tissues from the box on the end table and

hands them to her and takes one himself and gently wipes the tears off her cheeks. He continues quietly, "That's understandable. I mean that; I really do understand. And I respect that. You gotta know, I'm not saying any of this to try to hurt you; nor am I trying to belittle what you had with Michael in any way. There just is no other way to explain what was going on with me."

"I didn't tell you what I was feeling, Nikki, when I should have, because what I just told you about complicated matters for me. Eventually, it complicated matters for us. This morning when you woke up, you'd have known where you stood, and what my feelings for you were without a shadow of a doubt if I hadn't been wrestling with all this beforehand. It kept me from saying what I felt, when I felt it…when I should have told you but couldn't."

"That's what was messing with my head, interfering with my perception of what I was feeling. It was as though I couldn't let myself acknowledge the feelings that I was beginning to be aware of, because somehow, I thought I shouldn't be feeling them. Now that I had a handle on the issue, I could deal with it. I figured, alright, tomorrow's another day, let's see what it brings. I fully intended to pay attention to anything and everything that happened the next day, soak up every word and event like a sponge, and at the end of the day, I'd squeeze out what I had gathered, and then I figured I'd find my answer."

Nikki sniffed, and blew her nose. "My God, you do over analyze everything, don't you? Jesus Christ, Adam." He looks at her closely, answers her gently, "This somehow surprises you? Many times, doing that has saved me from an untold number of serious mistakes I could made, but didn't, because I took the time to think them through." 's voice returns to a tone more like his normal voice, "After I sorted all ut, I was rather pleased with myself, and not surprisingly, was able to fall ."

Nikki looked sadly and regretfully out the window. "I never r the storm. After what you just said, I'm sorry I didn't. I guess I was I fell right asleep." She looks back at Adam a bit self-consciously, "I u don't think I'm an emotional basket case, because I'm not." She ers, "At least, I don't think I am."

Adam gave her hand a reassuring squeeze. "Now, I never were. No need to be defensive at all."

"I do have to admit to being sentimental." Nikki offered certain commercials do me in. I've always been a big mushball." Nikki at the damp tissues in her hands like they were old friends, but she had become tired of their company. Adam was not at all surprised by her admission.

"Bah, you're just kindhearted. Not like me," he playfully exaggerated, "a grouchy old curmudgeon."

She smiles, and stands up, taking the wet tissues and throwing them away. As she walks back and sits down, she says accusatorily, "That's what you want people to believe.   I never did buy that about you."

"That's because I never acted like that with you." Adam replies, "You saw me act that way with other people, but not when I interacted with you. Oh I tried to at first, but your BS meter shot off the scale and you called me on it. It was less work to just give in, so, I caved." Adam shrugged and looked rather pleased with his explanation.

Nikki looked him in the eye and told him bluntly, "Oh, you're so fulla shit." She grins at the look on his face.

"No, because somehow with you, I didn't feel like I had to throw up that shield. I could be myself, all unvarnished."

She smiles and picks at a loose thread on the hem of her shorts. "So, that's why I'm special, huh?"

"Yes," he agrees, "among other things."

"All unvarnished, kinda like me, right now."

Adam raises his eyebrows, "What? Oh, you look fine. The question is, do you feel fine?   Considering what I was just talking about, are you ok?"

Nikki looks resigned, "Yeah, I am. Well, as ok as I can be about it. Look, I'm always ok with the truth. You can't help what you feel. Believe me, I know. It's knowing what it is that your feeling that sometimes isn't easy. Once you do know, how you handle it; now that can be difficult. Like with you, Mr. Sponge." She teases him gently. "You want me to believe that you were going to just do nothing, and see what happened with, of all things, your feelings?"

Adam looked at her with all seriousness, "Hell, yes. Like you said, and it's very true, you can't help what you feel. And I intended to see if I was correct in my personal assessment. Once I was sure, and if I was right, then would come the hard part."

Nikki's voice was hushed as she quietly asked. "And what would that be?"

Adam leaned forward a bit and responded in the same tone "Finding out if you could possibly feel the same way I do."

She looks at him in amazement for a moment, then chuckles.

Adam looks a bit puzzled, "What's so amusing?"

Nikki puts her hand on his leg and states, "You really couldn't see the forest for the trees, could you?"

"Not when I was busy over analyzing things, no. Damn, did I say that out loud? Forget I ever said that."

"Not a chance." She laughs and knows he won't admit missing anything, but he shrugs and agrees with her.

"Ok, I'll try to live with that. Meanwhile…" Adam acquired a patient look. "…I'll continue to answer the question at hand. Which, for the sake of continuity, I'll remind you that it was; when did I know that my feelings for you had changed." He looked tenderly at her, but also with a bit of reprisal for his earlier shortsightedness being revealed.

"Oh, thank you. Like I had forgotten." Nikki gave him a sidelong glance. "I was beginning to wonder if you had forgotten or hoped that I had."

He smiles indulgently. "Oh, no. Not quite, my dear, not quite. So…the next morning," Adam went on, happily explaining what his role in the day had been, "I knocked on the bedroom door at 5am, as promised. I didn't expect you to be Miss Sunshine at that hour, and I wasn't disappointed. Well, frankly, neither am I, so no big deal. We just stayed out of each other's way as we got ready to go."

"Before I dropped you off, I asked when you needed to be picked up. You said you could call a cab, but when I just ignored that, you told me 5 o'clock would be fine. I asked if you had dinner plans, and when you said no, naturally I asked where you'd like me to take you to dinner. I did mean it when I told you that if you had some friends that would like to come along, that it would be cool with me. You looked at me with an odd smile and said, "No, I'd rather keep you all to myself."

She said quietly, under her breath, "There's a tree."

Adam stopped and looked at her quizzically. "Pardon me?"

She waved her hand gesturing him onward, "You know, seeing the forest…? Never mind. Keep going, keep going, sorry I interrupted."

He gives her a sidelong glance, "yeaaahh."

Then Adam looked contemplative. "When you answered me like that, Nikki, I just wasn't sure how to respond. But what I was sure of was, after you said it, I was happy that you answered me that way. And that went a bit further toward my discovery of the night before and that maybe, just maybe, there really was more going on here with you, too."

"You could have just asked me…"

"Oh, right. Sure, and then you'd bolt."

"I would not!"

"Well, I had all day to think about what to do. The more I did, the more questions I came up with. It was getting harder for me to escape the conclusion that I really did feel more for you than I had thought I had before you arrived. Now the question was, how do I tell you that? And more importantly, what would you say? What would your reaction be? Because, like you, I worried about the very same thing you mentioned a while ago; what if I tell her what I'm feeling, and she backs away?" Adam explained, but with a worried, introspective expression. "Would it be worth the risk?" He turned his head, so his eyes could hold hers as he said slowly, "The more I thought about it, the more I was convinced that I had to risk it. I was faced with this fact; if I didn't find out in the next few days, I might never know."

"I decided that I wasn't going to kick myself forever because I missed the opportunity to tell you what I was feeling. The worst thing that could happen would be that you'd tell me you didn't feel the same way. If that were the case, then I doubted I'd lose your friendship. The worst I'd have to do would be accept the situation for what it was and go on.

Adam paused and grinned slightly, "I kept coming back to what you had said before I dropped you off and wondering what you meant. Did you mean, that you knew the things we'd be likely to talk about might seem strange to other people? Maybe, especially the gamer talk. But, could it be that it was more than that? What if you wanted to be sure you and I could be alone? I hoped that might be it." Nikki bit her bottom lip, and Adam looked a bit embarrassed.

"Then, I wondered, how am I going to do this? I'm no Romeo, by any means. Ok, I'll take her to a nicer restaurant, one that more fits the mood I'm trying to create. And I sincerely hoped that I hadn't taken complete leave of my senses and was about to do an absolutely crazy thing."

She smiled and poked him in the leg, "And what's so wrong with that?" Adam looked at her a moment, then carefully said, "Easy for you to say. Besides, remember, we're talking about me here. Well, ok, us, but my perspective on the events." Nikki was pleased with what she heard so far, and smiled encouragingly, "You seem to be doing just fine." Adam chuckled, "Oh, now I am, but then? Far from it." She told him sagely, "It's that control thing you men are cursed with." Adam looked agreeable to that, "Probably. But, Nikki," he looked at her with tender sincerity, and spoke quietly, "In a way, you're so very correct. You have to understand how different this was for me. All day long at work, I'm the go-to guy, the decision maker. I assess situations and make decisions that affect hundreds of people in the company, and our clients, with far less trepidation, and with far less self-doubt, than I was able to deal with what my own heart was telling me. These were my own feelings; and I realized I needed to be just as decisive about my personal life as I had been with my business life." Nikki nodded and smiled ever so slightly, "Ah yes, you finally had to be honest with yourself, about yourself." she said in a silken voice, "How I know the feeling." Adam nodded, and gave her hand a squeeze. "Right there," he waved a finger at her, "is just another reason why I love you." He leaned forward and gave her a gentle kiss on the lips. Nikki chuckles and gives him a slight push and grins, "Later...go on with your story." Adam hesitates, considering, then grins at her and continues.

"So, I get to the Center's parking lot just before 5 o'clock, and I'm guessing you're going to come back out through the doors you went in. I get out of the car to wait. It was such beautiful summer day. So, I decide to just enjoy the sunshine, and light up a smoke and wait. Then, I see the doors open, and a whole mess of people pile out of the building. Then I see you, talking with a few folks, and laughing. While you're talking to them, I see you looking around, presumably for me. Then you see me, and you flash me a smile.

Oh, my God. You're not going to believe this, I'm not even sure I believe it. When you threw me that smile, out of nowhere I felt like I had been shot right in the chest. I couldn't breathe, and my heart was going about ninety miles an hour. For a minute there, I thought I was having a heart attack."

He chuckles ruefully, "You know, people talk about being shot by Cupid's arrow, and now I know where they got that analogy from. I swear, that's exactly what happened to me. After my heart slowed down and I could breathe again, I just felt giddy as hell. I just couldn't keep this big 'ol smile off my face. If in any way I wasn't sure before, I definitely knew then. No doubt about it. I knew right then and there; I was falling in love with you." He looks thoughtful for a second, "Either that, or it was that horrible burrito I had for lunch." Nikki looks surprised, then scowls in mock annoyance, "Jesus Christ, maybe it was, you asshat." Adam pats his stomach and looks apologetic, "Naw, I got a cast iron stomach." She rolls her eyes, but then looks at him with concern. He sees the look, smiles, and chooses not to comment.

Adam holds up his index finger, "...and something else; I waited for it, but it didn't happen. There were no feelings of misgiving this time like there was the day before. No second guessing myself. It seemed I had come to terms with my, oh, subconscious kibitzing?" He shrugged, then leaned back on the couch and sighed in satisfaction. He waved his hand at her gently in an all-encompassing gesture. "I started to notice everything about you, not just notice, but drink all the details in like I was hyper aware. Like I said, I was one huge sponge."

"You finished up your conversation with those people, said your goodbyes and started walking my way. I took the opportunity to observe your approach. You sure noticed and gave me a "what the hell" look. So, I explained by looking you over, head to toe and back again and then I whistled at you. I could be mistaken, but I believed you blushed a bit." Nikki looked toward the ceiling and then back at Adam, "I just might have. I thought you were trying to be funny. That look of yours was so deliberately exaggerated...I thought you were just goofing around and giving me grief because I had a suit on." Adam shook his head, "...and you wonder why I was worried about how to tell you." "Pfffft, " she intoned, and then looked at him with amazement "You thought acting like a dog and wolf-whistling at me was a good start?" Adam tried to look contrite, "I did open the car door for you. I kinda liked doing that." She looked exasperated, then they both laughed. Adam's eyes glinted as he kidded her, "I was merely showing you my appreciation, but you know me, I just couldn't be serious about it."

"I figured you'd want to change before dinner, so I drove us back here. I made some coffee and put on the news. No real rush to go. I had already made reservations. Then I wondered if now the time was to try to tell you; but if we started talking..." Adam laughed at himself, "To tell the truth, I was hungry, and I also didn't want to miss getting to the restaurant in time for our reservation." Nikki gave him an exasperated grin, then looked away and laughed, which made Adam laugh, too. Then he grew serious, and looked around the apartment as he said, "The thought did occur to me that you might feel uncomfortable if I started to explain how I felt here in the apartment." Then he looked at her in concern, "I was worried that you might feel cornered, being here on my turf, so to say. I thought it might be better if I brought this subject up in a public place. One with the suitable ambiance to set the mood. I really didn't know how you were going to react to what I wanted to tell you; Hell, I still didn't know how I was going to tell you yet. I hoped that maybe the proper venue might give you a clue, and hopefully give me some inspiration, rather than to be here and just come out of the blue with it."

Nikki slid her back over until it was against the armrest of the couch, then stretched her feet out until they were near Adam's legs, but she didn't want to crowd him. Adam gave her an, "oh for crying out loud" look, and reached down and gently lifted her legs a bit and straightened them so she could stretch out, thereby setting her legs across his lap. Adam began to absently rub his hand slowly up and down her shins. She smiled at him and said, "You never seem to have a problem with words...it's one of your admirable qualities." He countered, "I do. I do when something that means a lot to me personally depends on what I say, and how I say it." Then he smiled, looked at her legs, then up to her face and sighed just slightly. "You're making this a bit difficult." She smiled sweetly and said quietly, "I'm just a little tired, is all." Adam nodded, and let his head rest on the back of the couch while he idly caressed her legs.

"The restaurant seemed like a good choice; not too crowded, low lights, candles, nice tables, pretty view of the city. Not a place I'd usually go." She smiled, knowing that was true, "I have to admit, I wondered if you'd even been there before." Adam considered, then affirmed, "Actually, no. But I had heard it was very good, and it was close to the Plaza, so I could show you around there after dinner."

"Of course, I was thinking about just how I was going to bring this up. I figured an opportune moment would present itself eventually. We were talking about our day, and that lead to other subjects; it's just so damn easy talking to you. So easy in fact that we were almost through with the meal, and here I still hadn't managed to bring up the subject yet. It's funny how when something is so important to you, it becomes more difficult than it needs to be.

As usual, I was enjoying your company. Just having you there, talking with you, and better still being able to look at you when you spoke. I started to notice the subtle things like how and when your expressions changed when you talked, how you used your hands; I also remembered to take a good look at your left hand." She raised her eyebrows. Adam shrugged, and then held out his hand in a gesture of clarification. "I knew you enjoyed wearing jewelry, but I was looking to see if you wore a ring that bore significance. I really didn't have a reason to look before; but now I damn sure did. I figured what I saw there might tell me something I might have overlooked, or something you neglected to mention to me since in all honesty it wouldn't have been any of my business." Adam tried to look neutral about that but failed miserably.

Nikki nodded, looked down and said softly, "So you were looking to see if I was involved with someone? You don't think I would have told you about something that important in my life?" She raised her eyes slowly back up until they met Adam's, and he returned her look unwaveringly, and said directly "You mostly likely would have, yes. I seriously doubted you had become involved with anyone. To be honest, I wanted to see if you still wore your wedding ring. If you did, it could mean that you might not be ready yet to hear what I wanted to say. It would have told me right there that I was going to have to tread even more carefully than I already had been. Nikki," he said emphatically, "I had to know, for both our sakes. So I could know what to say, and how to say it. You do understand that, don't you?" She nodded easily, "Yes, of course I do., and then she shrugged. "I just thought that was something all single men checked out whether they were interested or not. Out of habit." Adam replied a bit indignantly, "Maybe if I were the kind of man that was on the prowl. That's just not me. This had to do with you, only you and hopefully, with us. I'd like to think I was intuitive enough to be considerate of your feelings, no matter what I wanted." He looked at her until she smiled again, and then he smiled easily and relaxed a bit.

She sighed, and then leaned up and moved her legs so she could sit next to him, and then kissed him softly on the lips. "I'm sorry. I didn't mean to lump you into some sort of generic male stereotype. When it comes to you, I should have known better." Adam looked a bit sheepish, and shrugged slightly, "Oh, I have my moments. In fact, I had one in that restaurant that very night. Oh, wait, and the night before, too." She blinked in surprise, tilted her head asked quizzically, "Oh really?" Adam nodded solemnly, and said evenly, "Oh yeah, big time." Nikki scratched her head, then pulled on his T-shirt sleeve and wheedled him gently, "Like what? What happened; what did I miss?" Looking a bit uncomfortable, he nonetheless grinned ruefully, as if he was remembering something he rather enjoyed.

Adam raised his eyebrows, and then tapped her on the knee gently with his left index finger. "I'll tell you one thing you miss, and that's how often folks look at you, but I notice." He relaxed his hand, but let it rest there on her knee. "I suppose you'd call it a guy thing; checking out the room, the vibe, seeing what's between you and the door, if there's any mischief going on, or anyone that looks like they might be trouble. That kinda thing. Maybe you got all those looks and glances from folks because they'd never seen you around before, but I doubt it was only that."

"The night before when we were out, I saw a couple of guys here and there looking you over. To be expected. I just caught their eye and stared them down, and they got the message real quick. No need to bring it to your attention. But there was this one yahoo; I had been watching him for a while. He had been looking at you far too frequently to suit me as it was, but it was the way he looked at you spelled trouble in my book.

You had gone to the ladies room, and of course I watched you walk the whole way over there. Then I saw dumbshit get up and walk over to the ladies room and then stand near the door. I decided to take a stroll over there myself. I walked up to this guy and stood right in front of him, looked him in the eye, and asked him if he had gotten lost. He told me no, he hadn't, so I informed him, maybe he should consider doing so, before things got ugly. Then he made the mistake of saying to me, "Hey, man, what's it to you, she's not your wife." so I knew the son of a bitch wasn't even smart enough to try to play it off." Adam grew less amused and more serious as he looked at Nikki and told her, "My reply to that was, "What she is to me is none of your business, and if you want to walk out of here in one piece, then what she is to you is nothing. Comprende, mi amigo?" Adam's face regained a mildly amused appearance as he said, "He suddenly remembered he had to be elsewhere at that particular moment."

Her eyes widen in amazement as he relayed this new information. "Wow, you never told me about that!" Adam shrugged a bit, and laughed, "What was there to tell? Nothing happened, as intended." "Jesus," Nikki said, and looked at him with a slightly new perspective. "I wondered why you were outside the door when I came out; I just figured you were ready to go." He smiles warmly and shook his head, chuckled then gave her a hug. Then Adam looked at her, taking her all in, and then he sighed, his tone becoming more serious. "You really, honestly, have no idea how often men look at you, do you? You genuinely don't know how amazing you are." She makes a scoffing noise. "Me, amazing? Come on. I don't consider myself amazing, or anything special to look at, either." Adam just looked at her, "Well, think again. I can see if I try to tell you how attractive you are, you're just going to argue with me, and I'm not going to let you do that. You're just going to have to trust me on this one." He patted her knee gently, then began to caress her leg absently while he spoke.

"I suppose you could chalk that episode up to me simply being protective. I could tell that guy was going to be a nuisance. I was just glad it didn't happen in front of you. Because if it did, and if he were stupid enough to try to touch you, by the time I was done with him he probably would be wishing that I had just killed him instead. But last night, it was a bit different."

Adam took a breath, then shook his head and told her, "Sitting about two tables behind you there was this guy and this woman. The woman's back was toward us, but the guy was at the opposite end of the table facing us. Now I caught him giving you the once over, too." Adam shrugged slightly in resignation, "Ok, it happens. Once. Maybe twice, I'd give him.

This douche was staring at you half the time, the other half of the time he was making eyes at the lady he was with. He never once looked at me, and that was deliberate. Ok, new girl in town and all that, yeah."

"But it's what I was feeling that was important here, and what I was feeling was this; if I caught this guy staring at you one more time, I was going to have to go and break his face for him. Thing was, other than leave the place before we were ready, there wasn't a whole lot of peaceful or subtle options left open to me. Starting a fight is not what I came in there to do, by any stretch of the imagination; far from it. Plus, I was even more irritated than usual at the guy because this bozo was distracting me from my mission of the evening.

Then sure enough, when they were bringing us coffee, damned if I didn't catch him at it again. I felt the muscles in my legs tighten up to push back my chair and just before I got up to have a word with the fellow about his manners, he looks right at me. Then he looks at you, looks back at me, and nods his head and smiles. Adam shook his head, "It was like he was just letting me know he approved of my choice of companion. Then he goes back to talking to his lady friend like nothing ever happened."

Adam laughed quietly at Nikki's startled look, and told her, "Ok, maybe the restaurant idea wasn't such a good one after all. And not because the setting was wrong; it was perfect. It was my reaction to things that were bound to happen when we were out together, and that told me volumes."

"I know you might be thinking this is all macho bullshit, but it's the cause of that reaction that's crucial to understand. Especially with me. Without giving it conscience thought, I was ready to fight for you; literally. On more than one occasion in the past two days. The very fact I had such a strong gut reaction and it so easily overrode my natural tendency to over analyze a situation told me two things. Obviously, that I cared about you and was being wildly overprotective, but secondly, and more importantly, was that I still needed to know how you felt about me. Basically, I had to get my shit together." Nikki looked at Adam quizzically when he said that, so he raised his eyebrows and explained deliberately, "I have no doubt that it was my insecurity concerning our relationship at those moments that made me want to keep any other man that showed the slightest interest in you away from you, with force if necessary. I really honestly have learned not to be the jealous type; it's not worth it. If I knew that you felt the same way towards me that I felt about you, then I'd be secure in that knowledge and those things that set me off would never have bothered me. Amuse me, yes, and then I'd tell you about it and we'd both have a good laugh." Adam blew out a breath and reached for a cigarette. As he lit it he told her, "Now, I not only wanted to tell you, I needed to tell you how I felt about you as soon as possible for both our sakes, and soon, before you ended up bailing me outta jail."

Nikki was wide eyed, but quiet. It was very interesting to her to hear his side of events that transpired; things she had been unaware of until he told her. Adam seemed very comfortable sharing all this with her, and that made her feel very special indeed. She knew that he just didn't talk about himself out of habit. He was telling her all of this for her sake and to some extent for his own. She grew to appreciate that fact, and Adam, even more as he went on with his explanation of his perspective of their time together.

Adam put his feet on the coffee table. "It seemed I now had two missions; to get the hell out of that restaurant, and to find someplace, and some way, to tell you. I kept waiting for the right moment to just magically appear, and it just wasn't happening. Well, if it wasn't happening, then I needed to make it happen, somehow." He laughed and spread his hands, "Which was what I had been trying unsuccessfully to do all evening."

Nikki tweaked him a bit, "Don't think that I didn't know something was on your mind. I just had no idea there was so much going on; but then with you I should have known better." Adam told her with a small degree of irritation mingling with humor, "You know, you could have helped me out at any time. You could have just told me how you felt about me and put me out of my misery." She almost grinned and laughed softly, "I could say the same thing about you." Adam looked a bit exasperated, "Right, which is why we've been up half the night talking." Nikki rolled her eyes, she was getting tired, and when she was tired, she got irritable quickly. She sensed Adam was getting irritable too, and she didn't want this to degrade into a fight, so she spread her hands and said, "Look, if you don't want to talk anymore, you can stop whenever you like. You're not on trial here; you don't have to answer any more questions or say one more word if that's what you want. I can go to sleep, right here on the couch, in fact."

Adam blinked at her with apologetic surprise. "Hey... I didn't say that, now, did I? Come on, Nikki...relax." Standing up, he takes both coffee cups into the kitchen while Nikki rolls her eyes at his departing back. Shaking his head and reminding himself to tread carefully, Adam refills both cups, and returns to the living room. He puts both cups down, then sits back where he was on the couch. Adam's blue eyes show his concern as he smiles at Nikki. "Hey, I'm sorry. I think I've learned by now, if talking is what's called for, then talking it shall be." Adam smiled apologetically and shrugged his broad shoulders. "Like talking to you is a burden, anyway, silly one. Now where was I? Oh yes, outside." Shyly allowing a smile of appreciation to show, Nikki settles back to where she was on the couch before Adam stood up. He grinned at her as she tentatively laid her legs back across his lap. Beaming at her, his smile bursting across his face, Adam slides his arm across her legs and holds onto her. Both of them smile, chuckling at their awkward timidness together in person.

"So, I walk with you down the street to the Plaza, where all those shops and cafes border that huge square with fountain in the middle of it. Lots of folks gather there to shop, eat casually, or just hang out. It's way too social there for me, so I usually avoid the place entirely, but I thought you might get a kick out of seeing it." "I appreciate your sacrifice." Nikki told him, bowing her head graciously, "It's a very lovely place, Adam." Adam scowled slightly. "Yes, and full of people. And as we found out, full of people that work for me. I really wasn't expecting to run into anyone that knew me. I hadn't given that a thought. Not that I go out much, but apparently, they do, and it was obvious that my being there was a surprise to them." Nikki decided to tease Adam a bit about his anti-social nature. "Aww, they were glad to see you." Adam then redefined his statement. "They may have been surprised to see me; if they were glad to see me it's because they saw me with you. They finally catch the boss out in public, and with a woman, no less – what a coup."

"And every one of them we ran into asked me who you were; they never saw you before, were you from out of town? Where did you come from, how long have we been together?" Adam groaned and told her, "I had to tell them we were just friends because I hadn't yet gotten a Goddamn chance to ask you about perhaps changing that status." Nikki can't help but laugh at Adam's dilemma as he tells her about it. "Oh, laugh; it was just killing me. You were standing there, all smiles, hearing me say, no, actually protesting over and over that we're just friends, when that was the last thing I wanted you to think about us anymore..." Adam emphatically said. "I didn't know how much more I could take, then thank God along came Evelyn and they all scampered off. At least I was glad for a minute or so, before she lit into me, too. And as you've heard already, she wasn't buying into the "just friends" excuse one little bit." Adam looked at Nikki, who was still chuckling, and said sarcastically, "I guess I could have spared myself some trouble, and when those folks started asking me about you, I could told them something like, "This is the love of my life". She tilts her head and narrowed her eyes, "Oh yeah, right. Overkill. Like they'd have believed that considering you'd never mentioned me before. Oh, I have no doubt you would have done it, but then would I have believed you later?"

Adam nodded and pointed at her, "Exactly." Then he smiled and shook his head. "The thing that amazed me though is that Evelyn just seemed to hone right into the heart of the matter. I tried to tell her the same story, too. That we were just friends, and that you were visiting from out of town, nothing to it, really. I guess she could see in my eyes that I was lying through my teeth. She really did tell me that if I didn't do something to change our status from being simply friends into something that was in her opinion more appropriate, then I truly was an idiot. I guess she got all bold because we weren't at work, and it's a damn good thing she was right, too, for her sake."

"Captain Hard Ass rides again." Nikki intoned and then shook her head and lit a cigarette. "Yeah," Adam looked at her with some surprise, and then said with some frustration, "but this Captain was tired of beating a dead horse. I was beginning to think about giving up on the public venue thing, taking you home, and maybe when you were in the bathroom, slipping a note under the door telling you I loved you and then running away. If you screamed, I'd know that perhaps that wasn't a notion that you found acceptable." Nikki tapped her chin with her finger, then pointed at Adam, "That would have worked too." Adam lets his torso fall back on the couch, "Aww shit, NOW you tell me?" They both have a good laugh, then Adam shakes his head and sits back upright. The he looks at Nikki with open affection. "Naw, that wasn't going to cut it." Adam smiles, then sighs.

The Adam snapped his fingers, leaning forward and laughing again. "But, oh my God, then Jonathan showed up..." She grinned at the memory, and they both looked at each other and dissolved into helpless laughter. Nikki wiped her eyes with her fingertips. "Oh, that was classic you, alright. Set 'em up, then pull the rug out from under them." Adam chuckled, "Yeah, right? Goddamn that was funny. Not only was it funny, but it gave me an opening, and by God I took it." Adam then shook his head at Nikki, "And I didn't set up anything; you just being there was all that was necessary for Jonathan."

Nikki put out her cigarette and curled up next to Adam on the couch. He put his arm around her and smiled at her. He loved it when she laughed. "So he thinks he's the local Don Juan, eh?" Adam rolled his eyes and said quickly, "Oh God yes, he makes folks at work nuts with his stories. And this was such the perfect scenario; I couldn't have planned it better if I tried. All those folks from work just hanging around, but you know they were still watching you and me...trying to figure out just how fulla shit I really was..."

60

"When Evelyn pulled me aside to offer me her grandmotherly advice in private, I had no idea how long it was going to take. I didn't want to rude to the woman, but I had something I had to do, dammit!" Nikki chuckled softly. This was how Adam told stories online when they had a break in the action and it was so nice seeing how animated he really was when he got going. "Well, rather than just be rude I gave in and let her bend my ear about how dense I was being. I just knew this was gonna happen, but it couldn't be helped. Once I was pulled away from you, the crowd from work descended on you." He hugged Nikki and gave her a kiss on the forehead, "You were so brave. Poor darlin'." Then he laughed and she giggled back at him. "It's ok. They're very nice people. They probably wanted to be sure I wasn't a gold digger or something even worse. Believe me, they asked a lot in that short period of time. What you should be worried about, is what they told me about you." She grinned mischievously up at Adam and he laughed back at her in surprise.

"Now, that's funny, because before yesterday, they didn't know a damn thing about me that I hadn't planted in their heads myself. After yesterday, the one thing that they all knew about me for sure, or will soon know about, is something very important to me; you." Adam gives Nikki a quick nod for emphasis, then says, "I can see what they were hoping for, alright. Strange beautiful woman shows up from God knows where, spirits their evil boss away and bewitches him; then he becomes besotted and returns to work a happy man, and then they can all go back to work and screw off all day and he won't care. This, fortunately for them, is pretty much the truth." Nikki chuckles, and while Adam may think like that in jest, she knows when it comes to business he takes no nonsense. Well, she considers, maybe that's going to have to change a bit, now.

"So while Evelyn was advising me on my future, and about twenty paces away my dear co-workers are peppering you with questions, along comes ol' Jonathan. He sees you as a new yet unidentified target, and schmoozed his way right up to you. Well, the other folks just back off and give him room, because," Adam smiled and said with emphasis, "they know. Every one of them looked over at me with an "oh my God" face on, all except for ol' Jonathan. But I knew his deal. He was too busy trying to hit on you to notice anything or anyone, let alone me."

Nikki rubs Adam's hand, and then holds it and gives it a squeeze, "I'm sure he thought he was being charming. I could tell all those other people knew him, but I had no idea…" Nikki let her voice trail off. "All things considered, I tried to be nice." Adam looked at her dubiously,

"Oh yes, I could tell, no doubt in my mind. I could tell by the tight way you were smiling. You were being extra sweet, and not to mention the fact you avoided eye contact with me altogether. Smart lady, but see, I know you. Better yet, I know your voice, all one thousand variations of it. And I'm learning fast about your eyes. While your lips were smiling, your eyes were clearly saying, fuck off, toad. It was hilarious."

"The rest of the folks, they all knew Jonathan had just stepped into a big steaming pile of crap, and they weren't gonna help him one bit. In fact, they were just waiting for the show to get started. I bet they had no idea just what a show they were going to be treated to. Nikki smiled at him softly and said playfully, "Neither did I." Adam looked at her wistfully. "No, I bet you didn't."

"Evelyn, God love her, took a step in your direction, but I put my hand on her arm, stopping her. No doubt she was going to lecture ol' Jonathan about how inappropriate his actions were; but I was sure what I was about to do was going to be an even better lesson." Adam's blue eyes twinkled with mirth, and Nikki could tell he so loved telling her his version about how their meeting evolved. Nikki was enjoying not just hearing him, but this time seeing him as he told his tale. This time, however, she was the topic, and so far she was enjoying it.

"I crossed my arms and stood there, watching you both, waiting to see if ol' Jonathan would somehow miraculously figure out he was being a total ass and knock it off. I saw the crowd from work off to the side, whispering furiously amongst themselves. I knew this was going to be legendary."

Nikki smiles sleepily and ran her fingers gently over Adam's cheek, "Admit it Adam; you loved that, didn't you?" Adam turned his head and kissed her hand quickly. "What, that half my architectural crew was standing there watching this? Damn right I was aware of it, because I was going to have to live with what happened next every day at work. Did I love it? It served its purpose, and even better, it had the unforeseen benefit of helping me a good bit forward with the evening's original mission."

"I could have stood there a while longer." Adam shrugged. "Either you'd eventually walk over to me, or Jonathan would see me and perhaps wonder why I looked so unhappy. I just didn't know which was going to happen first." Adam looked at Nikki, and smiled in sympathy at her past plight, but then his smile became fixed. "That was my plan, until I saw the plan needed revising." Adam went on, but his voice changed as he recalled the event he was describing, and he said a bit tightly, "I saw you take a step backwards, and instead of giving you space, Jonathan moved up even closer to you and that's when I began to move. That was enough for me. Now I was thinking, what was going to bring this punk down a few pegs, but in a way that would keep me from losing my job and ending up in jail all in the same night?"

Adam couldn't help but grin and laugh a bit. "Inspiration struck with about my third step. It was pure genius. I walked directly over to you, put my arm around you, pulled you close and gave you a big kiss right in front of the amazed, and now obviously scared shitless, Jonathan."

"I thought I'd lay it on thick, so I said, "I'm sorry I took so long, darling, there was a line....well hello, Jonathan, I didn't see you there; how you doing, buddy?" Nikki giggled sleepily, and Adam was totally smitten. It was the sexiest sound he'd ever heard in his life. Nikki smiled up at him, and Adam grinned back happily. "Oh yeah, the look on his face was worth a week's salary, no, a month's salary. By the way, I didn't miss the look on your face either, but I already knew what I was going to do about that, but in the meantime, I knew I could count on you to play along.

"Then ol' Jonathan said..." Adam tried, not too successfully, not to laugh. "I'm doing good, boss. In fact I'm glad I ran into you. I wanted to tell you that I was going to be at work very early tomorrow to clean up all those little jobs that needed to be done. Maybe I'll wash the dumpsters, and yeah, the parking lot needs those lines repainted...maybe even the septic tank needed cleaning out. I'll be on all that starting tomorrow, boss, you can count on me." And then he hightailed it outta there. It was all I could do to keep a straight face until he was gone."

Then I felt you shaking, and I thought, "Oh, jeeze, now I've gone and done it." I tried to look at you, but you had turned your face into my shoulder and for a minute there I thought you were sobbing. Then I could hear you laughing; no, you were actually whooping with laughter. I put my arms around you and held you and laughed my ass off right along with you. God I hadn't laughed like that in a long time." Adam chuckled, "I looked around, but all my co-workers had buggered off, no doubt to call everyone who wasn't there and relay the whole thing to them."

Nikki looks thoughtful, "I wonder if that's what Evelyn took pictures of..." "Now there's a thought." Adam said almost seriously, "If she did, I'm going to have to find a way to give that woman a raise. Those pictures I would personally have blown up to poster size, frame them and put them in the break room myself." They both laughed again, and then Nikki sighed, "I wish I'd have known for sure he worked for you when he started in on me." But Adam quickly said, "Oh no, this was better. Because you had no time to think, it gave me no time to think, either." Nikki looked at Adam with a bit of surprise, "Yeah, and if you thought about just giving me a kiss like that earlier, you might have spared yourself a lot of angst." Adam smiled and shook his head in the negative slightly, "Ahhh, but I didn't know that, did I? You might think I am, but believe me, I'm not that bold. Which brings me to the next part of our evening."

Giving Nikki a bemused look, Adam continued "Here we are, standing in the middle of the Plaza, still in each others' arms. I really didn't want to move, but I had to do something, so I start to walk to where the cafes are, and somehow I managed to still keep one arm around your waist. Interestingly enough, you also had an arm around my waist, and it didn't seem that you were going to let go anytime soon, so neither did I. It was an odd start, but I'd take it.

I was just about to tell you how nice it felt to hold you in my arms, and then you stopped and asked if I heard music. I looked around, and it seemed there was a festival down the block, so we headed down that way. Inside I was cursing at that music for interrupting me, but soon enough I'd be thanking it as a blessing in disguise.

As we walked your arm slid downward, and I thought that maybe you weren't comfortable with your arm around me after all. Like you were trying to remove your arm without being too obvious, so I let my arm slide down too."

"Man, I was bummed." Adam looked at Nikki and she fondly smiled back, knowing what happened next. "I was thinking of some contrived offhand remark to explain away having our arms around each other. Like it was just an accident of some sort; nothing to worry about. Then as we walked, your hand lightly brushed mine. It was sheer reflex that made me close my hand around yours, and when I realized what I had done I looked at you, and I saw you smile. It was a look very similar to what I saw on your face after I kissed you. It made me smile, too."

"Then some song I barely remembered started playing and when you heard it, you stopped walking and got this look on your face." Adam looked at her tenderly. "I could tell that song really meant something to you; your face just lit up with this beautiful smile. You saw me watching you, and then you looked all sheepish and told me it was one of your favorites.

Then the light bulb went off, and I thought, "Oh, thank you God, thank you, thank you." Music had come to the rescue and become my salvation." Nikki chuckled and still looked a bit embarrassed by the memory, and Adam said, "When I said to you "Come on" you gave me this blank look, and I didn't think you'd go for it. So, I felt if I explained by telling you "Dance with me. It's my favorite song, so, we have to." you'd get the idea. I thought I was going to have to drag you out there." he said in exasperation. "I didn't know you liked to dance." Nikki tilted her head and raised her eyebrows. "Well, not particularly, but in this case, I was motivated." She looked a bit skeptical. "You could have fooled me, you dance very well." Adam explained with exaggerated patience, "I never said I didn't know how to dance, just that I don't usually. This was a nice slow rhythmic song, very sexy. In fact, it seems, it turned out to be the perfect song for the moment."

"It's funny, but there must have been a hundred people standing around, and I just didn't care. I put my hands on your waist, you put your hands on my shoulders, and there was that smile of yours again; except this time, I was ready with a smile of my own. Then you looked up at me," and Adam's voice got softer. "I hoped you understood what you saw there." Nikki caught the change in his voice and searched for something in his in his eyes. She whispered, "I thought I knew." He smiled and kissed her hand.

"But then after a bit, you moved closer and put your head on my shoulder. I wrapped my arms around you. Ok, no protest. Soon, you moved even closer. I sighed, and held you a bit tighter, closer. I was so happy, and I wondered, was this really happening? Well, you know me. I had to ask, "Would you do me a favor", and you looked up at me, all curious. Oh, the look on your face....when I said, "could you pinch me, because...well, because I think I'm dreaming"

You laughed and put your head back on my shoulder. Oh, what I was feeling at that moment. Like it was the most perfect time in the world." Nikki pointed out dryly, "Then you got a little bold." Adam looked surprised, "Well, can ya blame me? Now come on..."

"Yeah, into, what was it, the second song, a bit faster one, but somehow we didn't seem to break the rhythm of our first dance. I could smell your hair, and feel it on my neck, and my face. Not to mention a few other things of yours I was acutely aware of feeling, and pretty soon, you were about to feel something too, but unless we stopped dancing like that; there was no hope for it. She smiled in a relaxed way, "That's only natural, considering the circumstances."

Adam looked dubious, "Well, that may be true, but before I was faced with maybe having to explain why something had, shall I say, come up, I thought now was my chance to tell you; I better be clear on exactly what I was feeling. Finally, this was the moment to tell you. I was thinking, ok, easy does it, I didn't want to break the mood. I would have had to move a bit more than I wanted to, to kiss your cheek, so…since it was right there, I couldn't resist, so I kissed the back of your neck."

"I felt you shiver. Well, the sun had gone down a while before," Adam teased her, "and it wasn't as warm as it had been, but I rather hoped that reaction wasn't weather related. I held you tighter for a moment and nuzzled your neck some more. I have to admit, I was enjoying what I was doing, and speaking up right then just left my mind. Then you began to back up a bit. I felt this sinking feeling then, like oh, boy, here it comes, she's gonna tell me to cool it.

Then you turned your head so you could see me, and you just gave this look, and I was a coiled spring, just waiting to see what would happen next. I had expected you to say something, but then instead, you kissed me."

He chuckled ruefully, "Yeah, I'll be dammed, you kissed me. Boy, and what a kiss that was. I just so totally fell into that kiss, even my knees felt a bit like rubber. Like a schoolboy stealing his very first kiss. And yes, there was that heart pounding, lightheaded feeling all over again."

Yes, she remembered that moment. They had been standing there looking into each other's eyes, asking questions…looking for answers; the world around them forgotten. "Go on with your life" had echoed in her mind, and for once in her life she allowed herself to react instinctively to what she had been feeling. In fact, she smiled to herself, she went a bit farther than she ever thought she'd have the nerve to go. She was about to tell Adam that, but then he started speaking again.

Adam said with relief, "I was so tongue tied; thank God you spoke first. His face took on a wistful expression as he repeated Nikki's words; as if she didn't remember them, "I think I've seen enough of the town tonight; perhaps there's something else you'd like to show me?" Adam sighed and said with a bit of wonder, "Without another word, we started walking arm in arm toward where we left the car." Nikki had to fight to keep from laughing. Not at Adam being let off the hook by her reaction, but because the reason she didn't say anything was that she couldn't speak even if she had wanted to at that moment. What she had done scared her to death, and what she had said? She still couldn't believe she had actually said that, even when Adam repeated back her words to her, she still was amazed.

"And that's when I should have been talking." Adam said in self-accusation, "but you didn't say anything more, and I just hoped I was following your lead." Adam then said quietly and apologetically, "I didn't realize I was taking anything for granted by not saying more before we got here. I thought I was just letting you set the mood. No one knows better than I do, how hard it can be to say some things out loud."

She chuckled, then Adam's voice changed, and it became a bit too surprised to suit Nikki, "I have to admit, you really did surprise me."

She was lighting a cigarette but stopped with her lighter open. "I surprised you? How is that? Or should I ask, which time?"

Adam looked a bit defensive, "Well, you kissed me. I had kind of thought that it would be me trying to find a way to kiss you first, is all I meant."

She lights her cigarette quickly and then says with an amused look on her face. "You trying…" Nikki was almost sputtering, "You trying to find a way to kiss me first? What in the hell are you talking about? You did kiss me first, in fact, the first and second time! You kissed me twice, before I kissed you."

Adam looked like he was trying to remember, then he said, "Twice? Oh, that one with Jonathan. Well, yeah. But that really didn't count. Mind you, I don't regret that it happened that way one bit. The way it happened was, well, unique, but like I said before, it gave me an opening that somehow I had been too much of a dullard to find by myself all night long."

"Look, since it ended up as part of me getting the better of Jonathan, and not a deliberate part of me trying to tell you I loved you, then what does it matter? Can you understand why I might not count that as an official first kiss?"

She gave him a dark and what he came to know as a dangerous look. He drew in his breath; if a thunderstorm could be personified, then it was sitting in front of him right now. Note to self, never, ever, never ever again make light of anything that's precious to me.

Adam considered that thought. Precious to me? Yes, this woman is precious to me; he knew that now more than ever. One thing he did know, the intensity level of their relationship was too new between them to take anything for granted. He wasn't sure what just happened, but he was going to find out and not let it go until things were smoothed over; and by the looks of her right now, if he didn't repair the fuck up he just made, he was going to lose this woman. It might even be in the next few minutes if he didn't get control of this situation very soon. Adam was about to ask Nikki what had upset her so much, but Nikki saved him the effort.

She was smiling thinly as she spoke, her voice absolutely dripped with venom. "I'll have you know, that was a terrific kiss. Absolutely wonderful. Seemed sincere to me. Even considering the circumstances, as far as I could tell, it sure seemed like you meant it when you kissed me. I wonder, Adam, did you fool me?"

Adam about did a double take; what the hell did she mean?

"And whether you are aware of it or not, that kiss that meant so little to you was a major turning point for me. I had been wondering, just like you, if I had been reading things the way you had really meant them, or was it just hope or some sad desperation on my part. Despite what was going on all around us, you managed to plant a kiss on me that made me want to remember again how it feels to be with a man. How pitiful did you think I was?"

"What the hell are you talking about; you're pitiful? In no way did I ever think such a thing!"

She made a face of disgust, but then one of disappointment took its place. "I thought that kiss revealed a lot about how you truly felt about me. I had thought maybe even there was a chance you loved me, and now you're blowing it off as nothing? Now are you telling me you didn't mean it?

Adam began slowly, "A chance? Wait a minute; I didn't say I didn't mean it. Sure, I didn't plan for it to happen that way, but once I started kissing you, dear heart, I was not holding back one bit. I'm no actor. That was a certified real kiss, delivered by me and in public with witnesses. If it makes you happy, then yes, I'll admit that it was our first kiss. And therefore, yes I kissed you first."

Nikki counted off the events on her fingers, "Well, let me see, first you said it was part of getting the better of Jonathan, so in your opinion it didn't count. Now after seeing what you said annoyed me, you so casually decide to lie to me and say it does count to make me happy. What the fuck is that? Ok, so if I wasn't there, would you have handled the situation the same way? Would you have kissed one of your co-workers to have made that point?"

Adam states incredulously "What? Hell no!" He stands up and paces the length of the coffee table. "It happened the way it happened because it involved you, only you. If you remember, it was you he zeroed in on, and it was you the whole episode was centered around. If he wasn't trying to put the make on you, and in front of me, the whole damn thing would never have happened."

Nikki said very quietly, "Which whole damn thing? You kissing me in the Plaza, or us ending up in bed?" Stopping in his tracks, Adam spun on his heel and looked at her in amazement. Adam spoke softly and very deliberately. "Kissing you in the Plaza, under those particular circumstances. Good God, woman, I wanted to kiss you. I had been trying to find a way to tell you I loved you for hours. If that whole scene didn't happen yesterday, but happened two months from now, after you already knew how I felt, it likely would have played out the same way. I can't change when it happened. Ok, so I didn't really handle the whole situation very adeptly, and for that I'm sorry. It didn't end up so badly did it?" He smiled, but she wasn't smiling. He was missing something here, but what?

"You amaze me." Nikki said dryly, "All this time you say that you spent trying to find a way to tell me how you felt. How about asking me how I felt? If that was too hard, how about noticing how I felt? Good God, I thought I was being obvious as hell. What about how I reacted to you all night long? How about not thinking about yourself all night and open your eyes to what was right in front of you?" Adam paused and then told her truthfully, "I did notice, eventually, and I hoped I was right. I didn't want there to be any misunderstanding."

"You were surprised that I kissed you, let's look at that for a moment. Just how the hell can you be surprised?" Nikki laughed in disbelief, "You kissed me on the back of the neck! Adam said quickly, "I wasn't sure how you'd take it." Nikki raised her eyebrows, and said with exaggerated patience, "There is only one way to take it. In case you didn't know this, I'll clue you in. Friends don't kiss friends anywhere on their body that is ordinarily covered by clothes. That's one hellova indicator right there. I may not be the most experienced woman in the world, but some things are just universal. To most of us anyway."

Adam was still standing, and he spreads out his arms and leaned forward for emphasis. "Then how could you not have known what I was feeling? How could you not have known what my intentions were?" Nikki's voice was low, but it shook with emotion, "Oh, my dear, I knew what your intentions were. While we danced, that became so obvious. The intent on your part was clear. I knew where it was going to end up, and it may shock you to know that I didn't mind one bit. Oh yes, the intent was clear, but the context, that wasn't clear at all."

He blinked, "Context? Context of what?" "The context of that kiss on the back of the neck," she explained, "were you being romantic? Yes, you were. But again, the intent was clear, but not the context." Adam sighed, "You're going to have to help me understand a bit better what it is that you're upset about, Nikki, because right now, it seems like we're arguing about the fact that we do both love each other." Nikki leaned forward. "Ok, I'll try to make it simple for you. When we were dancing, I felt your arms tremble when they tightened around me. Did you think you could hide how your heart was beating? Did you think I couldn't recognize passion? Don't you think I knew what you wanted? The question was, exactly what was this going to mean? To tell you the truth, at that moment I didn't care, because God help me, I wanted the same thing. And I felt guilty as hell about it too. But if that's what you wanted, to knock off a quick piece, to just get laid…"

Adam looked horrified and told her, "Oh my God, Nikki, will you stop it?" But Nikki shrugged and said bitterly, "….well if that's what I had to do, to clue you in on how I felt, then by God I'd be the easy mark you wanted, just like that other chick you raved about…."

Adam held up his hand, and said sharply, "Ok, stop, just stop right the hell there." He waited to see if Nikki was going to allow him to respond to her, and when she sat there motionless and silent, he told her firmly, but calmly, "The intent was to show you what I was feeling, and the context that you questioned was about you and I, only you and I. Don't make the mistake of comparing yourself to anyone else I have ever known, because there is no comparison. Don't bring anyone else into what happens between us. What happens between you and I is all about us, only about us, and no one else. In my mind there is only you. Nikki, my God, I refuse to believe you are this fired up about who kissed who first. There has to be more going on here with you. What I'd like to know, no, what I deserve to know, is what in the hell is really bothering you?"

Nikki looked with quiet defiance into Adam's eyes, and then with steel in her voice she questioned, "All I want you to answer for me right now is, are you as capable of lying with your body as you are with your words?"

That brought him up short. He didn't expect anything like that. Adam paused, and looked at her in amazement. If there could possibly be a downside to knowing him too well, that was it, and she had just called him out on it. But this was totally different. This was about intimacy between each other. She was talking about the online crap. The joking with other people, playing with them; people he didn't give a damn about. But lie to her?

s, about us? Never in a million years. He took a moment, seeming to gather his thoughts and his control, then Adam said carefully, "Tell me at precisely do you mean by that?"

Nikki suddenly looked very tired and defeated. Adam just desperately wanted to gather her up in his arms and comfort her, regardless of whatever the hell it was that set her off. He knew that would be the absolute wrong thing to attempt to do right now, so he stood there in silence and waited for her to speak. When she did finally answer his question, she spoke very quietly, and calmly. "I'm tired. I can't do this anymore. You keep answering my questions with questions and…arrghh!" Nikki tossed aside the pillows she was leaning on and jumped up off the couch. Waving her arms to emphasize her words, she paced to the opposite side of the room.

"This whole conversation tonight has not been about words, it's been about actions, your actions, your feelings, and your explanation of them and how they pertain to me, and to us. And to why ending up in bed was the beginning of something wonderful, not just a means to an end. Adam, you said I know you, and how well I do know you." Nikki chuckled sardonically, "And I know you love to fuck with people. I always thought that when you did that to other people, it was funny as shit; but not when I think I'm the target of your fun! I'm going to tell you right now what I'm afraid of, not that I'm saying I think this is true," Nikki qualified, "and I'm not accusing you of this, so don't fly off the handle, but the thought has crossed my mind, ok? I'm only here for five days. How do I know for sure that you're not playing along with whatever it takes to get what you want out of me, and then after I leave, miraculously you'll have second thoughts and recant your claims of falling in love with me? You'd have all the expected excuses! Distance apart, different lifestyles, pick one, or find more. Then, you'd just disappear, change your cell numbers, put me on ignore everywhere and cut me off completely…"

"Nikki…"

She was on a roll, and his plea to her didn't slow her down. "Or even worse, you could act like nothing's changed, and since you're so far away how easy it would be to laugh at me behind my back. Saying sweet sounding endearments to me, but not meaning a word of it, just like that kiss that meant something to me, meant nothing to you. Now seems to be the perfect time to ask you about it; is this what you're doing here?"

All Adam could do was simply stare at her, speechless at her tirade. He sat down on the loveseat with a thud. He put his head in his hands for a few minutes while she stood across the room panting from her effort. Then he quietly groaned and raised his head to look at her. His blue eyes glinted like glaciers and his face was like stone.

Adam spoke softly, but steadily and earnestly. "I t̶ need to stop. I think you need to think about what you've just said. ̶ou about what I've spent the better part of the night telling you. Telling y̶ about things I've never told anyone before; not only that but telling you n̶ own innermost feelings about each and every one of them. All of it so you'̶ know just how damn much you mean to me. I was trying so hard to make you not only understand how I feel about you, but even more importantly why I feel that way I do about you. I don't know what else I can do to make you understand that I love you. I was doing the best I could to make sure everything I had done would be the exact opposite of what you just practically accused me of doing. Everything I told you about, everything I said to you was the God's honest truth; none of my words were lies in any way, of any nature, at all, whatsoever."

Nikki didn't move, her feet were rooted in the carpet. She knew she said too much, but it was what she was thinking. Fuck being indirect; this was her heart she was protecting. Scared to the core, she remained motionless and stoically to see if he had more to say. She wasn't surprised that he did.

His eyes bore into her soul, cool blue and unwavering. His voice was quiet, but steady. She could hear it tremble just a bit and that almost undid her. "And then there's this; you asked me if have I lied with my body to you? Never! And I never will. Please never accuse me of doing so ever again. There is no other woman that exists for me now. It doesn't matter if you're here, ten thousand miles away, or even on another planet. I love you, only you, and it's you that I will give myself to, no other." Nikki took a deep breath, but before she could speak, Adam had more to say.

"And please, Nikki, don't dare belittle your self-worth in my presence again. Especially by stating that anyone in their right mind would have the gall to treat you in the way you described, with what I feel is the ultimate act of disrespect by claiming that they love you just to use you for their own pleasure, and then throw you away when they're finished like a piece of garbage. Why would you even think that? If I found out anyone else had even thought about treating you that way, I'd kill them. And it wouldn't be a quick and painless death, I assure you. And yet, you just sat there and said that the thought had crossed your mind that I might be doing exactly that?"

Adam ran a hand over his face, and shook his head slowly, then looked back over at Nikki. "But I did say something that was careless. I implied that a kiss I gave you, didn't count for anything. That was horribly stupid of me. I should have realized that at this time something this personal, and this important, you'd be a raw nerve about it. For that, my love, I don't know how I can apologize enough. I didn't mean ill by it, I was making fun of that idiot Jonathan, and in no way whatsoever did I mean to trivialize anything that happened between you and I… I promise, I swear to you, I may joke and play and tease, but I will never ever make the mistake again of making light about anything that has to do with our relationship."

"You said you were afraid that maybe I'd just disappear. I think that may be the very heart of the matter here, Nikki, simply that you're afraid. Not all that long ago you lost someone you loved, and maybe this is all happening before you thought you were ready for it, but the fact is, it happened. We can't help that. We can't reschedule our feelings for a more convenient or more appropriate time. We can't help what we feel, or when we feel it. Now you're feeling love again, but this time you're scared. Scared because you already know how much it hurts to lose someone you love. You're scared to risk putting yourself in a position to be hurt like that again. There are no guarantees in life, my darling. But please, don't close the door on what we have, because of what might be."

Adam sighed, then spoke in an even softer voice. "I know you must be very tired. A lot has happened in the past few days that we didn't expect to happen. Good things, even wonderful things, can be stressful in their own right. Add that to the hell you've gone through in the last 12 months, and yes, something's bound to give. I have no doubt that you're emotionally drained and physically worn down. And when people are in that state it's very easy for them to be brutally honest. Like you, I can deal with the truth, even if the telling of that truth stings a bit."

A tear slowly made its way down Nikki's cheek, and it was all Adam could do to make himself stay put and not run over to wipe it away for her. The feeling surprised him, but it also warmed his soul in a way he'd never felt before. All he wanted to do right now was make her feel better and to get that scared reproachful look off her face. "Part of this stress no doubt is due to me, and how I totally bungled such a simple concept as falling in love. I hope you won't hold that against me. I'm a man, I'm human; God knows I make mistakes, but I refuse to believe that falling in love with you is in any way a mistake. What I do think, is that if you shut me out because you're afraid you're making a mistake, then you may be walking into an even bigger one, and I can't allow you to do that to yourself. Not yet. Not unless I know for sure that's really what you think is best for you. But you won't know, Nikki, unless you're willing to give us a chance. Give me a chance, give us a chance, that's all I'm asking."

Still standing, Nikki still looked pale, but all the tension and anger seemed to have vanished; the storm that she was had subsided. She tried to put a brave face on, and said in almost a whisper, "I had to know, Adam. I know what I said sounded horrible, but please understand, if I didn't ask the questions of you and hear you give me the answers, then I'd always wonder, what if... what if I didn't ask." Nikki sighed, and again spoke quietly, "When too much remains unspoken, too much can be taken for granted, or taken the wrong way. I didn't want either of us to pay for being over cautious about what we should know, and need to know now, before this goes any farther."

"But there is one more thing, Adam," Nikki paused and looked up at Adam. "What you understood...about me; I'm not so sure I could have said it that well myself." Nikki looked self-conscience, and a bit embarrassed. "I didn't come here looking for all this to happen. No one, not even you, can be more surprised than I am. I did things I've never done before in the last few days and giving in to what I wanted last night...with you, it was so easy to do, but hard for me to own up to. Realizing what I was starting to feel, and then it seemed you were feeling the same thing; it was hard for me to believe this was really happening. It just seemed to be happening too quickly to be real."

She took a breath and let it out. "What I said in the Plaza, when we were dancing; I still can't believe I said that to you. But when it seemed you ...wanted what I did, I... I couldn't wait anymore." Nikki began to blush a most interesting shade of red; Adam noticed the flush ran down her neck and disappeared into her shirt. "Maybe if I did wait for you to say something first, I wouldn't have felt so screwed up when I woke up tonight. I guess I felt guilty about being... so terribly direct. Good girls don't do what I did, do they Adam?" She smiled at him as Adam began to chuckle. "Nikki, you're a lot of things; good in any sense of the word, when it comes to you, is an understatement." Nikki blinked sleepily at him and said, "You're an amazing man, you know that?"

He stood up and walked over to her. Adam smiled tenderly and reached for her hand. "And you're a very strong, intelligent, and sensitive woman. I've already told you you're amazing. But now I'm putting my foot down. You look tired as hell. We're going to bed, and you're going to get some sleep. I'll take no argument from you either, young lady." Nikki smiles shyly at him, and he gathers her in his arms and kisses her, gently at first, then thoroughly and passionately. When their lips part, Adam sighs and smiles tenderly. "And that's just a sample of what's in store for you, after you've gotten some rest."

Nikki smiles back at him, a bit more confident as Adam walks with her into the bedroom. He pulls back the covers, then turns off the light as she gets into bed. Carefully he spoons in behind her and wraps his arms around her, pulling her close to him in a warm, comforting embrace. They were sound asleep in a matter of minutes.

CHAPTER IV

The caress moved slowly and idly across her ribs to her stomach, over to her left hip, down her thigh, then slowly back up across her ribs. The pattern repeated itself casually. The touch was gentle and assuring. Nikki's eyes slowly opened and saw the bedroom ceiling, and she was aware of his body touching the length of hers on her right side. She turned her head and saw him lying there next to her, elbow on his pillow, head propped up in his left hand while his right hand continued its travels for a moment more.

"Morning" she said softly and stretched thoroughly.

He gave her a tender, amused smile. Adam leaned over and kissed her lips softly, then he told her, "I'm afraid we missed morning entirely, and a huge part of the afternoon. It's about…" he rolled over to his right to see the clock on the nightstand, and then rolled back to exactly where he was before. "Five thirty in the afternoon."

Nikki blinked. "You let me sleep that long?"

Looking mildly surprised, Adam told her, "Let you sleep? I only woke up about an hour ago myself."

She sat up and looked at him, considering what he said. "What have you been doing, watching me sleep?"

"Indeed, I have. Oh, I dozed off a bit here and there, but for the most part, yes, I was just laying here, watching you… looking at you. Thinking about how lucky I am…" His voice trailed off and he then shrugged slightly as he said, "There just isn't anywhere else I'd rather be right now." His face softened a bit more, and he traced a circle on her arm with his fingertips. "I wanted to be here with you, when you woke up." He looked at her with subtle meaning, and she gave him a look of understanding.

She nodded, knowing exactly what he was referring to; the

first time she woke up here in his bed.

Adam apparently was taking great care to be sure there would be no repeat in any way of that 'particular doubt' on Nikki's part.

She leaned over and kissed him on the forehead. Then she slid out of bed and headed into the bathroom. "Where do you think you're going? Oh…"

He started laughing, and she retorted laughingly, "I have to brush my teeth too, dammit."

He gave her a moment for privacy, then he rolled out of bed and following her into the bathroom. As she started to brush her teeth, he said, "Good idea." He came up close behind her and wrapped his arms around her and held her close to him as she brushed her teeth. He looked into the mirror over her shoulder at her and grinned. "Very good idea." She smiled as she felt his body pressed close to hers.

He let his chin rest on her shoulder and continued to watch her in the mirror. This was a good idea, for the obviously delightful reasons, and for some more practical ones. The lights over the sink were bright, and there was little in the mirror that could escape his notice, so he could satisfy his concern about how she was doing without having to ask her too many questions. It occurred to him that she wasn't acclimated to the altitude like he was, and no doubt that also contributed to her state of distress last night, but he wasn't going to point that out unless he saw any more obvious signs of exertion. He was glad to see she looked better than she had earlier this morning; she seemed rested and felt relaxed in his arms. Good, there were no dark circles under her eyes and there was a blush of color in her cheeks and lips. Her lips, Adam couldn't help but smile thinking of those lips. It had been a long night of talking, soul searching, and eventually love making.

There was no help for it; things had to be said out loud, listened to and examined by both of them. It was difficult, but necessary. He felt a twinge of guilt at keeping her up so long, and he considered how difficult coming to terms with all that was new must have been for her. It was new territory for him as well, but both seemed to have come through last night's marathon heart to heart for the better. For months he had worried so much about her well-being; if she was getting enough sleep or how she was managing her stress. There were times during their conversation he felt a bit hypocritical as they both indulged in a lack of sleep, not to mention some acutely stressful moments as the talking went on through the early morning, and the hours ticked by until mid-day. The ebb and flow of quiet conversation that occasionally moved into humor, which then became the emotionally charged moments, all made for one rather interesting evening. In fact, he realized it was the most captivating and fulfilling night he ever experienced.

All that transpired the night before seemed to have forged a bond between them he could feel tangibly. He had to admit, it wasn't just how he felt about Nikki, but how she made him feel about himself. There was something about her that just allowed him to open up to her, and in doing so he was able to look at himself in ways that he didn't bother to before. She had talked as much as he did, and what they had to say to each other had confirmed the way they both felt about each other, but not in the way she had first feared that it might. No, far from it. He smiled and kissed her neck, and she looked in the mirror and grinned back. What they had before between them had been nice, but this…this was indescribably wonderful. Moreover, because of that, Adam discovered these small everyday moments now all held meaning for him. The knowledge that the opportunity for these moments must come to an end in a few short days, no matter how temporarily he intended that to be, reinforced just how precious they were.

She smiled and handed him his toothbrush. "I can go make coffee," she offered. He paused as he put toothpaste on his toothbrush. "You realize it's almost six pm, correct?" She wrinkled her nose at him, "Of course I do, but there's nothing we can do about that now; I suppose I'm going to be entirely nocturnal for the rest of the time I'm here." Her smile became fixed and then faded to a sad grin. "I'll get dressed and make the coffee." He quickly replied. "The coffee, fine, but I don't know how I feel about that "getting dressed" part, though." She smiled back at him and walked into the bedroom and out into the kitchen.

As she departed the bathroom, he allowed himself to recall again that they didn't have that many days left before she'd be leaving. They just slept one of them almost entirely away. He sighed, and knew eventually they'd have to talk about that, too.

Adam thought about the small slice of life that happened between them a few moments ago in front of the bathroom mirror. He realized that's how he wanted his life to be, not just thinking about those moments but living them every chance he could. He smiled to himself; this was one project he didn't need a tickler file to remember to work on. Starting Monday, he'd be doing just that. But he'd keep that to himself for the time being. What he had in mind may take a while, if he could swing it at all. If that didn't pan out, there were other options, and he fully intended to explore as many as it took until he got what he wanted. He always got what he wanted. No, he admitted, he'd like to think he always did. He just tended to forget the times he lost, and never forgot the times he won.

It wasn't hard to find what she needed to start the coffee. After she ground the beans, and put those and the water into the machine, she turned it on and walked into the living room. The aroma of the coffee already begun to waft through the air as she walked to the window and drew the blinds enough to see outside. The mountains were visible from here; she hadn't realized that. The last time she looked out the window it had been dark. She looked at towering peaks in wonder. Midsummer, and still there were places that had snow up there. Snow, she thought with distain. I really have come to hate the snow. Thank God this trip wasn't during the winter months, but then again, this place could handle snow much better than D.C. That thought gave her pause. What about her; could she? Could she live in a place that snowed on average 55 to 60 inches a year? Now that might be a problem. Not that she especially loved living where she did but living here.... that would be tough to do. Then again, there were other things might keep her where she was; not that they didn't have a place in her heart anymore, it just was her heart now had more to hold. She sighed and thought about her work. Her career. Her job had gotten so specialized, there was little hope that she could find one in the same field or even something similar anywhere but in the D.C. area.

Ouch, she thought, I'm already making it sound as though compromise is impossible here. I'm setting myself up for a no-win scenario. Is this me being practical or overly cautious again? Well, let's not get ahead of ourselves; in six months Adam might get … The thought was one she couldn't even finish. Tired of her? Oh, give yourself some credit, and him too, you ass. Yes, how to handle this situation is going to come up eventually, she sighed, and sooner than she'd like. A shadow of a smile began. Nice try, lady. You know you're dying to talk about it with him. This would be a lot less complicated if you just accept what is, and not waste energy trying to imagine what might happen. Look at where you are now, and what you're feeling at this very moment. Did you even imagine that you'd be in this situation a week ago? Hell no, you didn't. So, making yourself crazy trying to think of everything the future can throw at you isn't going to solve anything.

Deep down there was no denying it, she knew she wanted to be with him, and she recognized what she was starting to do. In her typical self-depreciating way, she was building up a defense made of logical explanations so on the anticipated fictitious day somewhere down the road that this relationship would eventually end, then she could always look back on this moment and say, "see, you knew this would happen." If she got her defense down pat, and it all fell apart, then it wasn't going to hurt so much, was it? On the other hand, wouldn't it be safer and easier on the both of them to just stop this right here? Just call it a good time, thank Adam for a wonderful week, and leave it at that. Let poor Adam off the hook. Leave Denver without any hope or expectations of a future with him. She felt the tears try to surface, and she smiled sardonically. Ok, admit it, you know damn well you really do love him. You just can't whitewash over it and call it something else.

Then all the conversations of the past few days with Adam came flowing back into her mind. This was Adam and she knew him well. To everyone else he was the tough guy, the loner, the guy with a self-imposed impenetrable shield, and thinking back he had done everything he could possibly do to make it obvious none of that applied when it came to her. The man had said things to her that she never would have dreamed he'd be capable of sharing with anyone, and he told her without hesitation or being self-conscience. He didn't need to, but he had. And when she summoned the courage to come right out and ask him about what she feared the most, Adam had practically taken his heart and laid it out fully exposed on the coffee table to let her look inside it.

More than that, she knew the way he thought; in Adam's mind, when you know someone, you own them. In the process of telling her not only that he loved her, but why it was he knew that he loved her, he had given her knowledge that was tantamount to sole possession of his heart. He did it because he knew she needed to have no doubt about how he felt about her, and he spared himself nothing in the telling. My God woman, what else do you need him to do to let yourself believe in him? She felt a bit abashed, because if he knew what she had been thinking a moment ago, he no doubt would tell her she was being silly. Again. He'd be right, too.

It's too late for that, my dear, she lectured herself. You love him, and you know what you're going to go through because of that; a long-distance romance, that's what. She bit her bottom lip in contemplation. Now seriously, how often are you going to be able to fly to Denver? It wasn't the money, flights didn't cost that much really. It was the time involved. Six to eight hours travel time one way alone; no short weekend getaways. Well, no, maybe we could meet halfway sometimes. She had to stop herself from laughing aloud. Wasn't that the very essence of compromise, meeting halfway? This can work, if you allow it to. Hard doesn't mean impossible, as long as this is what you both want. Now, there's the true question, is this what he wants? No, the real question here is, am I what he wants?

Being so absorbed in her thoughts, she didn't hear him walk

up behind her until he was close enough to touch her. He wrapped his arms around her from behind her and looked out the window with her. She sighed, and he did too.

"I bet I know what you're thinking about," he said gently. "I have to admit, I was too. But we're not going to find the answer in a day, and since we don't have the days to spare, let's not spend too much time now trying to find the best answer for us."

"I love you." Nikki quietly spoke, feeling uncertain all over again. "As long as we both want the same thing, we'll try to find a way to work this out. Right now, I don't know exactly how, but..."

He smiled to himself. It was the first time Nikki had said to him "I love you". Well, in those exact words; he was well aware she had told him in other quite memorable ways. Still, this was a milestone for Adam and he privately cherished it. Adam loosened his embrace and turned her to face him. The smile he gave her melted her heart. "Then, we'll look at what we do know." Adam started to tick off the list on his fingers. "I love you. I love being with you. I want to be with you every moment of every day. Hell, even when we do live together, we'd have to go to work, and I'd even hate that time apart. But we'll do what we have to do, now, and then, too."

The use of the definitive 'when we do live together', not, 'if we live together', wasn't lost on her. Nikki wondered if that's what Adam really wanted, or if he was saying that because he could. After all, she had only said we'd try to work it out. Not that what he suggested was a bad thing to consider, but was it really possible he had already considered their future? She listened to him as he spoke again. "Then there's you," he continued, "I know that you love me. You know I make damn good coffee. I'll never complain about how much you game, because I'd be gaming, too. How could you not want to be with me?"

Recalling what she had been thinking, she wondered if somehow he sensed her thoughts and he had made it a point to ease her mind. Putting her arms around his waist, she pulled him into a hug, which he accepted and returned. He kept his left arm around her waist and with his right hand stroked her hair. "Don't dwell on the sad things my love," he said softly. "Always try to remember the good things. That will help us get through this, and we will make this work. You'll see."

They stood there in each other's arm for a while, neither one wanting to move. How ironic that he should say that, she mused. For the last few days every time they tried to think about being happy, some sad memory would come along and try to derail that feeling of happiness in one form or another. No, she corrected herself, we let it do that. Until yesterday; now we both know what kept haunting us. Time to let that old self-reproachful introspection go, lock it up and throw away the key.

Slowly they released their hold on each other, and they both looked out the window. Then suddenly she queried out of the blue, "Do you ski at all?" Adam uttered a surprised bark of laughter. "Hell no, I hate the cold."

Adam blinked and looked at her quizzically. "Do you?"

That made her laugh too, and she pointed at the snow on the mountain. "That's one place you'd never find me," she said and walked toward the kitchen. "I hate the snow, and I hate being cold with a passion."

He followed her into the kitchen, and as he opened the refrigerator, he laughed. "Why did you ask, then?"

She took two coffee mugs out of the cabinet and started to fill them with coffee. "This is Denver." She shrugged as though that explained it all. He glanced at her and grinned as he took out a carton of eggs and some sausage and set them on the stove. "And your point is that everyone who lives here is required to ski, is that it?"

She handed him his coffee, and she poured some milk into hers, made a face at him. "I was wondering what brought you here." Her gaze landed on the food he had taken out and put on the stove as he pulled out two frying pans. She looked up at him and raised her eyebrows. "Breakfast?" she intoned with an amused look.

"Well, we did just wake up. Besides," Adam tried to hide a grin. "Don't we have to consummate the ritual of love making by having me make you breakfast when we wake up?"

She lowered her eyebrows and shot him a look that made him laugh.

"Ok, how about this then, it's quick and easy, and we do have to eat. Is that somewhat less offensive, my dear?" She nodded in exaggerated satisfaction and sat down on a barstool by the counter.

"Now, as for how I ended up in Denver, that's just where the job happened to be. The company I work for is based here." He turned to look at her, his expression serious. "I'm not chained here for any practical or aesthetic reasons, if that's what you were asking. I just landed here and had no reason before recent events to consider changing that." He opened the package of sausage and rolled it in the pan, turning up the heat under it to medium, then looked at eggs and turned to her again. "How do you want your eggs?"

Nikki waved her hand in a dismissive gesture. "However you make yours; I'm easy."

He turned back around and pulled a bowl out of the cabinet. "You definitely are not easy, woman." Breaking the eggs into the bowl, Adam chuckled and shook his head. "Easy? Oh, my dear. Far from it. I'll have you know that you are complex, stubborn, willful, emotional, determined and demanding." Her jaw dropped as he turned around and faced her with the bowl in his hand. He started whisking the eggs and continued, ignoring her look, "You are also passionate, compassionate, intelligent, beautiful, alluring, generous, considerate, loving, did I say beautiful?" Grinning, he shrugged. "Ok, beautiful, giving, confidant, strong, sexy and vivacious. But easy?" he smiled tenderly at her, "No, you're anything but easy."

She picked up her cell phone and raised it up, taking a picture of him. At his look of surprise, she commented, "I wanted to capture this historic moment. Not only are you right, it seems you've finally said something that I can't argue with." Laughing, he walked over and kissed her. "Good. Try remembering that in the future."

Now that her cell phone was in her hand, she noticed the ringer had been set to vibrate, probably because of her attending the conference, but she had forgotten to turn the ringer back on. She frowned, and he noticed.

Mildly concerned he asked, "Anything wrong?"

She made a sound of annoyance. Christ, she had voicemail. "No, at least I hope not. My ringer was off, and I have voicemail…" She looked at the recent calls list. Both her daughters had sent her text messages. She read them first. Good, the girls just sent hellos and status reports on their doings, and reminders to pick up souvenirs for them. Although they were a tad old for that, she smiled indulgently and knew she'd get them a little something. Then she looked at the missed calls list. "Oh shit." she muttered. Adam turned quickly and looked her way. Anna had called. Not just once, but three times.

She started laughing, and he poured the eggs into the other frying pan, and turning the sausage over as he remarked, "I take it then, there's no crisis anywhere." "Well, my daughters sent text messages, keeping me up to date as usual on their adventures", she reported, "and reminding me to get them souvenirs."

He nodded as he stirred the eggs. "Sure, we can do that."

With a slightly embarrassed look, and a wicked grin she said, "I forgot all about it. I guess I got sidetracked, somehow." She could tell, even from behind him, that he was smiling broadly.

"However," he interjected, turning around and crossing his arms across his chest. "I seriously doubt that's what that "Oh shit." was about." His eyes settled on hers with a patiently expectant look.

"Well, I'll know when I check my voicemail. It's from a friend at work." He frowned. "She has called me three times." Adam started to chuckle. "You better call her back. She may have called the hotel you were supposed to have stayed at, and if so, then she is probably worried about you."

She hit the speed dial button for her voicemail, entered the required password, and listened.

He plated the scrambled eggs and sausage and set them on the dinette table. He walked over and took her nearly empty coffee cup and refilled it, and his, and then looked at her face. If he could read her look, and he was sure he could, she was catching hell in the voicemail message.

Nikki grinned, and then hung up. "You were right, I'm going to have to call her." She walked over to the dinette table and sat down. "After I eat."

Adam could live with that. Looking at his plate, and then at her, Adam admitted, "I didn't realize I was so hungry. I guess I was a bit preoccupied, myself. We do have to keep our strength up, don't we?"

"Whatever for?" Eyes sparkling with merriment, she became inspired. Picking up a sausage link, she looked at it, and then looked at Adam suggestively. Slowly she ran the tip of her tongue along the edge of the sausage until she got to the end.

Adam froze, his fork in midair, staring at her, totally enthralled.

As she reached the end of the sausage, she slowly surrounded the end of it with her lips, then slid the morsel ever so slowly into her mouth and then slowly back out. Taking a small bite out of the corner she looked at Adam with the most innocent of faces.

Adam was utterly transfixed. When he could move again, he made a small, quiet, strangled sound, and carefully put his fork down on his plate, then folded his hands on the table. Adam nodded toward what was left of the sausage in her fingers and in his best patient voice told her, "Do that again. But," he smiled slowly, "I have to warn you, if you do, then I predict your food is going to get very, very cold before you get a chance to eat it."

She started laughing helplessly at the look on his face.

"Not that that's a problem, mind you, we can always warm it up, or make more, personally I don't give a damn which." Adam continued, smiling broadly. "But there are two things I am compelled to point out that are of immediate higher importance to consider here. First and foremost, you do need to eat, and I'm going to see to it that you do eat, and rest, while you are here, and if it seems that you are indeed rested enough, then perhaps later I'll entertain that offer of yours." He was losing the battle at attempting to sound stern. "Secondly, before we get," Adam paused, considering, then said, "sidetracked again, you better call your friend before she really gets concerned and calls the police and has them go looking for you."

Wiping her eyes, she put down the sausage and began to eat the eggs. He chuckled and looked at her fondly. "Goddamn, you, woman. I love sausage. Now I won't be able to even look at it again without seeing you, seeing you do that." They both laughed and finished their meal. As he picked up the plates, he noticed that she hadn't touched the sausage again, and he smiled to himself as he cleaned up the kitchen. "Let me help with that." she offered. "No, you better call your friend." he answered, putting the dishes in the dishwasher, "This won't take long." "Alright, I'll call her now." She turned back to him, "Oh that reminds me, did you ever check your email? To see if Steven sent you those pictures?" He looked up, "No, I haven't," he smiled in remembrance, "We were busy. But thanks for reminding me." He started to wash the frying pans. "I'll check it as soon as I finish these up."

"If it's all the same with you, I'd rather stay in tonight. I know you're still tired," Adam began. Nikki looked about to deny it, but Adam would have none of it and continued, "What do you want to do? We could go game for a couple of hours... Might be fun, sitting next to each other while we played; our own private LAN party." Adam chuckled, and Nikki considered it for a moment, but then said, "I don't know, if you really want to, we can. It's just that, well, since we're here..." her voice trailed off. "You're right," Adam said, understanding what she was implying; soon enough that's how they would be forced to interact in the evenings, well, that and the phone. "Either way, whatever you want is ok with me."

She started to leave the kitchen, but then he called after her, "Nikki, are you sure you had enough to eat?" She stopped and slowly turned around, a sweet smile slowly spreading across her face. "Do you have any idea how it makes me feel to hear you say my name?" Then she caught herself and smiled sheepishly. "Anyway, yes, I had plenty, and thank you, that was very nice of you." Scoffing at the accusation of being nice, Adam had a point to make. "Well, you didn't eat much; you hardly touched the sausage." She threw him an impish grin. "I will, later...as soon as you say I'm rested enough." Now it was his turn for his jaw to drop as she turned on her heel and walked into the living room.

She detoured into the bathroom and brushed her teeth again quickly, then walked over to the breakfast bar in the kitchen and picked up her cell. Adam passed her on the way to the computer table, patting her on her bottom playfully as he went by, and then he pointed at her and smiled, as if reminding her he knew what she meant by the "rested" comment, and was going to hold her to it. She grinned happily, and fervently hoped so. Adam sat in front of one of his computers.

Picking up her cigarettes and lighter from the end table, Nikki lit one and sat down on the couch while dialing Anna's number. The phone only rang twice.

"It's about fucking time you called me back!" Anna shouted in greeting, "Goddam it, Nicole, where the hell have you been? I was about to call out the entire Denver police force and tell them to go find your stupid inconsiderate ass!"

Adam's eyebrows climbed to the ceiling as he peeked over his monitor at Nikki. Obviously, he could hear Anna all the way across the room. He tried not to laugh aloud. Nikki on the other hand, couldn't help but laugh and that just irritated Anna even more.

"Ok, asshole, what's the deal?" Anna demanded, biting off each word with acerbic brevity. "I called the hotel where you were supposed to be and they said you cancelled your reservation!" Nikki could tell Anna was just getting warmed up.

"Well, hello to you, too, Anna," Nikki said calmly, fighting the urge to giggle. "By the way, I thought that it was against the law to reveal that information. Or, for that matter, for anyone to ask for it."

"It is, you ornery bitch!" Anna hissed into the phone. "I lied and told them I worked for the travel agency. And before you think that's funny, I called from your phone on your desk."

Nikki sighed. "They can't trace through a trunk line, dumbass, so you're safe, this time."

"Safe." Anna squawked and then continued in a rush. "And that's another thing I was going to get to in a minute, but I don't need to now. You must be safe because you finally deigned to pick up the phone and finally fucking call me, so back to my first question, why did you cancel the reservation?"

Nikki finally raised her voice so she could be heard. "Anna, will you calm down a moment and let me tell you? That is, if you really want to know, and not bust my balls all night."

Adam smiled to himself with satisfaction. So, she did talk to all her friends like that and not just her gamer friends. Apparently, the three-dimensional types also possessed the capacity to respond in a similar nature. He shook his head with barely concealed humor. Anna had no idea he could hear her. This conversation was a riot. Women. you just never knew how they behaved without men around. That is, until you got the chance to eavesdrop on a phone conversation between two friends. Looking over his monitor again, Adam smiled reassuringly at Nikki who shrugged and grinned back at him. Yeah, Adam thought, he could get used to this.

Anna finally took a breath. "Ok, you can start explaining to me. I'm calm now."

"Hardly." Nikki sputtered at her friend but continued before Anna went off on her again. "Here's the deal, I was told the place was not only a dump but too dangerous for me to stay there, so I didn't. It's just that simple."

"You were told, not that you saw it for yourself, huh? Who told you that? Ok, wait a minute here, just where the fuck are you?"

Nikki took a breath and said to Anna firmly, "If you need to talk to me, call me on my cell phone."

"I tried that," Anna snapped back. "Several times, remember? All I got was voicemail and you didn't call me back, so I was getting just a bit goddamn worried about you."

"As I was about to say," Nikki continued, "You can call me on my cell phone. I'm sorry Anna, I had it on silent for the conference and I forgot to turn the ringer back on."

There was a loud snort heard from the other end of the phone. "You? You forgot to..."

Hurriedly Nikki cut her off but not before Adam fell into helpless but silent mirth behind his monitor. "I assure you; the ringer is on now and if you call and I'm busy, I'll call back when I can." Nikki smiled a bit and glanced at Adam, who smiled back knowingly. She could tell he was planning for her to be busy alright, and sometime soon.

Anna wasn't buying the simple answers Nikki was giving her. She knew something was up with her friend that she hadn't told her yet, but Anna was determined to get her to spill it. "The conference is over now, so just what the in the hell could you be doing that you'd be so damn busy that you can't answer the goddamn phone? And don't think I forgot; you didn't answer me when I asked where you were, either." Anna pushed her point onward. "Give, where are you, or I swear I'll call out the dogs and have you hunted down!"

Nikki sighed with exasperation at her friend's tenaciousness. "Anna, I'm staying at a friend's place. Really, you have nothing to worry about."

"A friend's place." Anna repeated dubiously. "You don't know anyone in Denver."

Nikki laughed despite her growing frustration with her friend. "Anna! You ask me a question that I don't have to answer, and when I do, you don't believe me. Do I have to remind you I have friends all over the world?"

While Anna thought about that a moment, Nikki got up and

walked over toward Adam, so he could hear what Anna was saying now that she wasn't yelling at the top of her lungs.

"Ohhh, you mean those people you play games with? Oh come the fuck on, Nikki. I suppose next you're going to tell me you met up with one of them, and it turns out he's some gorgeous guy and you're staying at his place."

Adam and Nikki looked at each other and tried unsuccessfully not to laugh. "As a matter of fact," Nikki whispered and let that statement hang there.

Anna's reply was instantaneous and succinct, "Bullshit."

"Ok, Anna," Nikki said dryly, "then I won't tell you. I'll let him tell you."

Nikki offers Adam her phone and he takes it, shaking his head with amusement, and then speaks into the phone with his softest dulcet voice, "Hello Anna, Nikki is indeed staying at my place. She's in good hands; no need to worry at all. In fact, I'm taking very, very, good care of her." Nikki sputters as he hands the phone back to her.

At first the phone is silent, then they both hear Anna scream. "Anna?" Nikki laughs into the phone, waiting for her friend to recover. "Are you alright?"

"Oh, my God!" Anna catches her breath, and she squeals again. "I'm doing ok," she remarked in a voice drenched in sarcasm "...but apparently not doing nearly as well as you are! Holy shit, Nikki, when did this all happen? And an even better question," Anna rushed on, "why the hell didn't you call me and tell me! Jesus Christ, Nikki!"

"I'll fill you in when I get back, Anna, I promise." She saw Adam was looking at pictures on his monitor, but she couldn't see them very well. "Anna, dear, if you're satisfied that I'm just fine now, I do have to get going."

Anna chuckles fondly at her friend. "Yeah, I just bet you do, you sneaky wench. Listen, Nikki, good for you, girl. Take some pictures, I wanna see this guy."

Nikki ponders that a second, "You know Anna, you may already have seen his picture. I can't remember. But I think I'll have some new pictures to show you when I get back."

"Well, alright, but can't you text me some now?" Anna wheedled "Nikki, come on, take a selfie of you both!"

Nikki hadn't thought of that, but then she remembered what they were wearing, which wasn't much at all. Looking down at herself, then at Adam, Nikki shrugged at their lack of clothing and Anna was nothing if not impatient.

"I think I can help." Adam whispered so only Nikki could hear him. She raised her eyebrows and looked questioningly at Adam and he turned his monitor so she could see what he was looking at. There were the pictures Steven had sent as promised, and there were a lot of them; she could tell by the row of thumbnails along the bottom of the screen. "Anna, you may be in luck. It seems one of Adam's co-workers sent him some pictures they took of us yesterday. Give us a minute and we'll pick one or maybe two to send you."

Anna perked up, "Oh, cool! I can wait." Then Anna purred into the phone, "His name is Adam, is it? How wickedly biblical and delightful."

Nikki groaned and Adam chuckled. "Shut it, you goofy bitch," Nikki fondly admonished Anna, "I don't want you scaring him off." Nikki looked at Adam with a slightly concerned expression, but he snorted and said under his breath, "Never." As she stood next to him and looked at the pictures, he reached over and ran his hand affectionately up and down the back of her thigh.

"I heard that," Anna practically sang into the phone, "God he has a wonderful voice; tell me girlfriend…" Anna dropped her voice suggestively. "What else is wonderful about him?"

Nikki blinked and said softly, "I don't have the time right now to tell you everything."

"Wow," Anna said dramatically, "somebody has fallen hard, haven't they?"

Nikki rolled her eyes, "Shut up, you, will ya, please?"

There they were, the pictures of both of them in the Plaza. Adam pointed to one, and Nikki smiled. It was of them dancing, but at a moment when they stopped to look at each other. His hands were on her waist, and her hands were on his shoulders, and they both were looking into each other's eyes intently. Nikki knew exactly when that moment had occurred on their fateful night of discovery, and she started to get a bit choked up. Adam knew as well, and he put his arm around her waist and gave her a reassuring squeeze. Then he tapped the screen and smiled at her. She looked, and it was a picture of them right after Jonathan had left them. They both were smiling; her arms were around his waist and her head still on his shoulder. He had his arms around her, and his eyes were sparkling with mirth.

Damn, those were good pictures. She nodded and typed in Anna's email address, attached the two pictures and grinned as she typed in the subject line "afk" and hit send. Adam saw and smiled as he held her close for a minute, giving her a quick kiss.

"Anna," Nikki said quietly, "you should have them now."

"I do," Anna confirmed, "they're loading." They waited, but not for long. Anna made a low whistle and said under her breath, "Wow. Ain't technology wonderful? Here I was all this time giving you shit about playing that game, and this is what came of it? Goddamn, I think I need to start playing some online stuff myself."

Nikki grinned and ran her fingers gently through Adam's hair and he sighed with delight at this new and delightful sensation. They looked into each other's eyes and were totally lost in the moment.

"Ok you two, those were nice, but where's my selfie?" They both jumped, startled by the intrusion of Anna's voice into their reverie. Before Nikki could respond, Adam answered in a stage whisper, making sure Anna could hear him. "We're not sending one, Anna. Sorry, but we're not dressed yet. I'm sure you understand." Adam winked at Nikki while her jaw dropped.

Anna squealed then giggled into the phone. "I bet you're not!"

Adam grinned up at Nikki, laughing out loud at the expression on her face. Adam put his forehead on Nikki's hip and chuckled quietly. "Anna, you realize I'll be dealing with you when I get back, right?"

Anna laughed again for a bit and then her voice got uncharacteristically serious. "Get back? What, you're kidding right? You're coming back, and leaving him behind? Girlfriend, you're nuts."

Nikki blinked and looked at Adam, not sure what to say. "Nikki, if you leave him out there, you're gonna lose him. There's no way a guy like that is gonna wait for you or anyone else, so don't take it personal."

It dawned on Nikki that Anna had no idea she was letting Adam listen in, but it was too late to tell her now, so she just covered her eyes and waited for Anna to finish. She didn't even want to risk looking at Adam yet. "Once you're gone, bang, you're history, honey. He'll be calling some other chick before you even get off the plane. You know that, don't you? Guys like that aren't for girls like us, you know what I mean?"

Nikki drew in her breath, and Adam looked up at her sharply, then at the phone with annoyance. "Anna," Nikki said weakly, "please, shut up."

"Well, alright," Anna retorted, "But don't say I didn't warn you. I'll talk to you later, and, good luck, girl. You're gonna need it." The connection ended, and Adam thought, not a moment too soon.

Setting her cell down, Nikki looked at Adam, still sitting by her side at the computer table. He was shocked to see that her eyes seemed haunted with sadness and regret. Whispering softly to her, he pulled her gently into his lap. "Come here, baby." She put her arms around his neck and laid her head on his shoulder and he put his arms around her and held her tightly, because he knew what was to come. It had to happen sometime, and her friends departing words had no doubt pushed just the right buttons to shatter any self-reserve that was remaining for Nikki to grasp. He knew what was coming was the proverbial "good cry", which he faced with silent resolve. It was an outlet, he understood that, and he couldn't deny her that. He resolutely prepared himself and when he felt her body slightly shake, he ruefully thought it should be him making her body react like that, not sadness or grief.

He could tell she was fighting it, so he whispered, "It's alright, Nikki. Let it go. It's ok to cry. I'm right here with you." Turning to face her he gently kissed her cheek. "I always will be. You're not going to lose me." Adam quietly insisted, whispering in her ear while he gently stroked her hair. "She doesn't know me, but you do. Nikki, I'd wait for you forever if I needed to, but I won't have to. We will be together. I promise you that." He held her tighter as the silent sobs came and racked her body. He knew it wasn't just what Anna had said; it was also everything else she'd been thinking about, and everything that worried her. After any emotional turmoil, eventually there had to be a release, and crying was nature's pressure release valve. That's why he wasn't terribly surprised when he felt his face damp with tears of his own. It pained him to hear her cry, but it killed him to feel her physically torn apart with sadness. He felt it too. He just thought his time would come after she left, when he was here thinking about her, alone.

Eventually, the heartbreaking sounds subsided. Adam could feel her chest rise and fall against his as her breathing tried to return to normal. He rubbed her back slowly as he held her, sometimes kissing her cheek, but saying nothing, letting her find her balance but supporting her in every sense of the word. Even in this role, he found himself happy, delighted to be there for her. He felt a sense of belonging, that her being in his arms was somehow not only right, but how things should be always.

Nikki lifted her head from his shoulder and began to lean back so she could see his face. Adam relaxed his arms to allow her movement. She looked at him, her face still wet with tears, and sadness still controlled her features. Nikki swallowed nervously, shook her head, and then said softly, "Adam, what are we doing?"
Adam knew what she meant but was at a loss for words.
"You tell me to try to not think about how we're going to handle this now, but it won't be any easier later." Nikki slid off Adam's lap. She looked at him and said each word deliberately, "Have we lost our minds?"

Nikki stood in front of him, and he could see in her face that she was struggling to say something more, so he waited for her. She finally spoke, but he could tell that she had to force herself to say the words. "I can't hold you to that promise, Adam. I was upset, and I know that's why you said what you did. You're very sweet for saying that, but how can you know what you want after just a few days together?

Adam looked calmly at Nikki and smiled. "I know I love you." He spread his arms apart and shrugged. "It's that simple."

The corner of Nikki's mouth pulled upwards in an attempt to smile, and she replied quietly, "As simple as the last three days, Adam?" She turned and walked away toward the kitchen.

Adam knew that those very three days that Nikki remarked on had not only been the hardest thing, but also the best thing ever to happen to their relationship. So far, he corrected himself. He knew what he wanted, now the trick was to make her see that.

He followed Nikki into the kitchen and found her pouring two cups of coffee. When she heard him behind her, she turned and smiled at him and handed him his cup.

Adam took it, gave her a smile, and then took her free hand. "Come on." he told her, and gently led her back to the living room. He stopped at the couch and simply said, "Sit." Nikki raised her eyebrows but sat on the couch anyway.

Adam put down his coffee on the end table, then put his hands on his hips and stood in front of her, looking at her with a combination of consternation and affection. "First of all, we are not losing our minds. If anything, Nikki, both of us may have just found some peace of mind, particularly," Adam emphasized his next words, "because of these past three days."

Adam put his hand on his chin, and looked down for a moment, then back up at her. "Let's look at this piece by piece; humor me, if you will, Nikki. You need to know I didn't make that promise because you were upset. Or," Adam looked a bit self-conscience and amended, "because I was. In fact, I don't make promises that I don't intend to keep. Ever. It's bad business, and that's one business habit that does extend into my personal life."

"I told you, I love you. You do know that now, don't you, without any doubts? Nikki, you do believe me when I tell you that, don't you?"

Nikki answered him slowly, "Yes, I do."

Adam nodded and then asked her bluntly, "Nikki, do you love me?"

She smiled and said quietly, "Yes, Adam. I love you."

Adam nodded, then said soberly, "Do you think when you get on that plane Sunday and head back east that my feelings for you are going to change once you leave here?"

Nikki looked stricken and hesitated. "I know mine won't. All I can do, is hope that yours won't either."

Adam sighed and said reproachfully, "Nikki, do you have that little faith in me? Do you trust me that little?"

Nikki looked uncomfortable, and reminded him, "Trust has to be earned, and faith? Adam, I believe you when you say this is what you want now, but what about after I'm gone? It's easy to tell me you love me when I'm sitting here in front of you, but what about when I'm not here?"

"You keep saying that." With an exasperated sigh, Adam walked to the couch and sat beside her. He smiled in understanding and took her hand. "I know what you're trying to do, but you can save yourself the effort. You're trying to save me from myself, and while I appreciate the thought, I know what I want, thank you. What I want, is you. Nikki, if I didn't want you to be a part of my life, I wouldn't be suggesting it." He smiled reassuringly at her and continued, "And when you love someone, the natural progression of things is needing to be with that person, and as much as possible. Are we agreed on that?"

Nikki nodded her head slowly in the affirmative.

"And what that means to me is that I want to be with you every morning, every night, every day of my life. How do I know that after just three days? Because I already thought about what it would be like to live without you." Adam looked at Nikki intently, "My reaction was as strong as yours was a while ago, believe me." He paused to be sure she took that in. "So, it's only logical to believe that we would want to be together more often, and eventually, in a more practical manner. Unless you tell me that's not what you want."

Nikki groaned and said, "But Adam, what I may want, and what you may want, is controlled by things beyond our control. Yes, I want to be with you. But damn that Anna, she made me think of all the things that could go wrong. Not just about what may happen between us when we're apart..." Adam gave her an annoyed look, but Nikki went on, "But about just what we'd have to actually do to be together. One of us, or even both of us, would have to uproot their home, possibly even their career. Adam, the thought of it is..." She looked down, braking eye contact, clearly in discomfort. "it's so overwhelming." She looked back up at him. "Don't you think I thought about what I could do, even though I haven't said anything to you about it? Adam, what I do, doesn't exist out here..." she let her voice trail off.

Adam never did ask her what she did exactly for a living, although he had an idea, but right now he didn't give a damn. He stood up and began to pace the floor. "Nikki, it's only overwhelming if you let it be. We need time to consider our options, and if there are no obvious ones, then we create an opportunity and make that option exist. Don't just let life run you over because what you want to do won't be easy. You have to take control and make it happen if you want it bad enough. You have to go on with your life."

Her mind reeled when Adam said those words; it almost felt like an attack of vertigo. Go on with your life. Once again, she was back at the cemetery, and she could plainly see Mr. Hodges turning toward her and saying those very same words. She shivered involuntarily and hoped Adam didn't see her. Nikki pulled her attention back to Adam. He was standing still and looking right at her, and when her eyes met his, he gave her a questioning look. When Nikki didn't volunteer anything, his appearance changed to one of concern, but he went on, "Nikki, I know you have strong ties to where you live, and it's not just your career." He wondered how far he should go with that, and decided to settle on, "There's your girls to consider, for one thing, and at this age, I know they need you to be near them." Then he chuckled ruefully. "Even if they don't realize it."

Nikki considered that as Adam walked back to the couch and sat down close to her and gave her a thoughtful look. "You mentioned uprooting a home." He looked around and gestured at the apartment expansively. "This is a nice place to live, but Nikki, not necessarily my home. Someone's true home is always where their heart is, and you, my dear, have sole possession of my heart." She smiled and he picked up her hand and kissed her fingers. "No matter where you are, my love, that is where my home is, be it here right now, or wherever else you are."

Then Adam sighed and that look of annoyance returned. "And as for what this Anna told you..."
Nikki quickly said, "Now Adam, I didn't say she was right, or that I believed her..."
Adam shook his head and said with intensity, "No, I didn't say that you did, and I sincerely hoped you wouldn't. But it does bring up one valid point, one that we've skirted around, but now I'm going to address it."
Nikki blinked and looked at Adam in surprise. "Ok, and what is that?"
Adam's face grew serious, and held Nikki's hand a bit tighter.

"What Anna did bring up, and in one dammed irritating way I might add, is the subject of trust. And, Nikki," his voice dropped down an octave, "don't tell me what she said didn't get under your skin." His eyes held hers in a gaze she couldn't look away from, but she couldn't say a word to rebut what Anna had said.

Adam went on in the same low, deliberate tone, "You answered her a while ago, you may not even know you had," he continued, "when you said that trust had to be earned. I can't argue with that Nikki, because it's the truth. But you have to give me the chance to be trusted, before you can feel that you do. All I want to say about that is give me that chance." He smiled and leaned forward and brushed her lips with his. "That's all I can ask. The rest is up to you."

"But Adam," Nikki pointed out, "I already gave you that trust. On several different levels."

He raised his eyebrows, pretending he didn't know that already, "How so?" Nikki tapped her chin with her finger, "Well," she considered, "when I first arrived here and you disapproved of my hotel, you told me I could stay here, and I did." Adam nodded, "That's true, you didn't hesitate. You know," he paused, "I told you before, I did wonder about that; the fact you agreed to come back here." Nikki laughed and tapped the tip of his nose with her finger. "It was because I trusted you." She smiled a bit and said, "You disapproved so strenuously about that hotel, and then offered for me to stay here; I had no reason not to, or to feel uncomfortable about it."

Adam decided to press the point a bit further, "Are you sure that was all it was, Nikki?" and he let the question hang there. Then he was sorry he asked. Nikki had already told him she didn't come here to pursue him, nothing of the sort. Who was he not to believe her? He realized too late that this question served no other purpose than to satisfy his ego. What did it matter what she may have been feeling for him before she arrived, when what was important was that he knew how she felt about him now. "Look," Adam reconsidered, and said quickly, "you don't need to answer that…"

"It's alright," Nikki said and held up her hand to stop him, and with an introspective look on her face she said quietly "You had to know I cared about you, but Adam, not like I do now, not then." Then Nikki looked at Adam with a thoughtful expression, and asked him, "Are you asking me if I loved you before I came here?" Now it was Adam's turn to look uncomfortable, and before he could respond, Nikki continued, "Adam, of course I loved you. If you had told me you needed me here, that you were sick, or hurt, and needed my help for whatever reason, I would have done everything in my power to be here for you. I'd have done it for you, but also for several other select people that we both know. If you're asking if I would have come back here with you in lieu of a place to stay if Michael were still alive, the answer would still be yes," she saw Adam try to hide his surprise, "but not for any more reason than a friend offering another friend a place to stay." She gave him a level look, "Because that's what we were, Adam, we were friends. Close friends. If Michael were alive, nothing would have happened between us. I know that, Adam, because I wouldn't have been able to live with myself if it did." Nikki smiled at the look on his face. "It's true." She chuckled at the look on his face, "Even if you professed your undying devotion to me as soon as you found me in the terminal, I would have had to tell you while that was very nice of you, that I was spoken for." Then Nikki looked embarrassed, "God, that was an unfortunate choice of words, wasn't it?" Adam chose not to comment and let that go.

      "It wasn't until after I was here, and the situation being as it was, during dinner that first night I began to consider just how much I did care about you, and I wondered what you'd think about that if I told you someday." Nikki paused, looking for the right words, "Once I started thinking that way, I started to…to see you differently than I had before. I felt guilty as hell about that, too, as I already explained to you. I don't know how else to describe it Adam, somehow, I just knew…I just felt…" and her voice trailed off as she saw she had made her point. Adam gently encouraged, "That, maybe, it was meant to be?"

      "Maybe." she said as quietly as he had spoken. She looked at him a bit helplessly and shrugged self-consciously. Then Nikki took a breath, let it out, and said resignedly, "Adam, that night in the Plaza…"

      Adam leaned over and kissed her again, interrupting her tenderly. "You don't have to tell me, Nikki. I already know." He smiled in understanding, but she still looked uncomfortable so Adam told her reassuringly, "Nikki, if for one moment I had sensed any hesitation or doubt on your part, believe me, I'd have stopped right there, and would have fell all over myself apologizing to you. The absolute last thing I wanted to do was anything that would have upset you, or made you feel uncomfortable." Adam's eyes danced a bit as he said, "And if I would have crossed the line, I'm sure you would have let me know in no uncertain terms that I had done so." Adam leaned forward a bit and said earnestly, "You have to understand, Nikki, this wasn't about just any woman that I was interested in. Because it was you, Nikki, if anything were going to happen between us, I had to be sure it was because I loved you. Not just because I wanted you."

      She looked at Adam with warmth and affection. Somehow, he found just exactly the right thing to say to her, and at exactly the right time. Nikki looked up at him from under her lashes, saying coyly, "That's not all I let you know about in no uncertain terms."

Adam laughed, "Isn't that the truth! "Good lord woman, when you want something, you certainly have a way of making what you want very clear, indeed."

Nikki huffed at him playfully, "Well, Adam, if I left it all up to you, we'd still be dancing in the Plaza."

"Oh," he chided, "I don't know about that. But you did make it very clear you were done with sightseeing for the night."

Nikki looked at him with an innocent face and said, "Well, not entirely...." as she reached for the waistband on his sweats and gave it a tug. "As I recall, there was a quite a bit more left to see that night."

Adam gasped, and then started laughing again.

"Tell me," Adam said through his laughter, "did I look as shocked as I felt? Because you could have knocked me over with a feather at that moment."

Nikki tried to continue to look innocent. "I had no idea I shocked you. That wasn't my intent."

Adam chuckled and pulled her into his lap. "Sweetheart, that was the first time of several times that night that you shocked me, and all of them were quite pleasant."

She raised her eyebrows and looked thoughtful. "You know, I should pin you down on that and make you explain that statement, but out of kindness I'll refrain from exposing what an obviously weak repertoire you must have if I shocked you that first night."

He started laughing again; oh, how he loved this woman. Making a face at her he corrected her, "I didn't mean bedroom gymnastics, not that anything we did would come close to that description."

"Well, then" Nikki asked as she ran her finger down his chest, "how would you describe it?"

He pulls her closer, his voice soft and seriousness. "The best way to describe that first night would be a very tender encounter."

Nikki looks at him and suddenly seems concerned. "Were you disappointed that it was like that? Did it have to be more?"

Adam looked at her in surprise, "No, God no. It was everything it should have been, no more, no less. It was perfect." Adam sighed and told her, "I don't think I'll ever forget that evening, that song, or that dance. I know I'll never forget last night, or," he looked at the clock, "was it this morning? Had to be last night."

Nikki's face took on an impish grin, "The second time, or the third?" Adam looks at her, smiles, and plays with the ends of her hair.

Nikki snuggles closer to Adam, then her expression changes.

Sadly, she sighs and says under her breath, "Time…"

Adam doesn't want to think any more about how little time they have left together; soon enough, but not now. He doesn't want Nikki to either. Perhaps a pleasant change of subject would help. Adam tells her in a contented voice, "I have a feeling anytime we make love, it will be perfect."

Nikki pulls back a bit and looks at him mischievously "If that's the case, then what do we have left to strive for?"

He smiles meaningfully as he lays her gently down on the couch, whispering suggestively, "How about we work on expanding my repertoire?"

CHAPTER V

The sun just started to illuminate the mountains, delivering the brilliance of a new day promised by the brightness of the early morning sky. The snow that remained on the peaks was awash in the pinks and purples of dawn. This was one of the benefits of being an early riser. That, and getting into work hours before the rest of the crowd filtered in. More was accomplished in these hours than the remainder of the day, especially when Steven visited and arrived early.

These early hours of the morning were also the time of day when power conversations were best received by his supervisor. Not so much because of the early hour, but mainly because no one else was around demanding attention, and today was no different. Just the start of another day at the office. Adam would rather think of several other things right now and allowed himself to do just that for a moment of self-indulgence while Steven finished reading a report.

Adam noticed a plane high in the sky, its contrails turning pink and purple as well from the light of the dawn. He smiled a sad, private smile. In the early morning, he always saw planes tracking across the sky on their way east or west, but he never used to give them a thought. He sighed heavily. Ever since Nikki had left, he now saw the distant airplanes as being filled with people that other people somewhere else loved. Maybe they were parting ways, or perhaps someone was coming home to a loved one. He groaned and made a mental note to thank Nikki for one more thing in his daily life that he could never look at the way he used to before he met her.

"Well, what's your take?" Pulling his attention back to the

matter at hand, Adam told Steven patiently, "Yes, we can send Jack and Bob to Japan for a meeting with Ingwa's brass. However, I submit to you again, why blow the thousands of dollars for plane tickets and hotels, when we have the capability for a videoconference right upstairs? If we were at the point that a face to face would be critical to our relationship with Ingwa, and they even seemed warm to our proposal I'd agree. Right now, I believe they're just using our company's interest as a litmus test for other offers. I don't feel we..." He paused; the cell phone in his pocket was vibrating, and it was set to do that for one person and one person only.

He glanced quickly at his watch. Damned early for Nikki to be calling, in fact she should still be on the way to work. "Excuse me one moment, Steven."

"Sure thing. Oh, and, tell her I said hello." Steven smiled and backed off a few steps, suddenly engrossed in the document in his hand.

Adam gave him an amused look, and then smiled himself as he answered his cell. "Hi darling, listen, can I call you back in a few minutes?" He heard the usual traffic noises, and some sirens in the distance. She hadn't answered him yet, and he wondered if he lost the signal.

Then he heard her make a gasping sound and say in a trembling voice that froze him rigid. "No, you can't call me back." she said in a strained voice, "...ever..."

His back straightened, and his heart began pounding. He heard sirens in the background, and then heard one so loud that he pulled the phone away from his ear. He could also hear through the phone people shouting in the background. Steven was also able to hear it, and looked over at Adam sharply, his amused and indulgent look turning to one of alarm.

"Steven," Adam said as he turned and hurried towards his office. "I have to take this call."

Steven stared after him as Adam walked quickly into his office, then pulled up a chair and sat down to wait. Whatever it was, it wasn't good at all, and he thought he better hang around and be here when Adam got off the phone.

Rushing into his office, Adam closed the door. "Nikki that was a damned odd thing to say to me; I hope you know that's not very funny."

Adam heard her laugh weakly, and take in a shuddering breath before she said in a thin voice, "Funny? No...not funny at all."

She seemed to be distracted; he thought again, no it was more than that, she sounded more like she was drugged. "Nikki, what's wrong?" Then Adam asked more gently, "What's going on there?" He began pacing.

"I don't know how long I have, Adam," she said haltingly and then she gasped again, "I had to call you, I had to tell you, I love you...while I can."

Her breathing was labored, and he heard her gasp again.

"Nikki, for the love of God," Adam implored, his voice growing stronger. "What the hell's going on there?" He heard more voices in the background now, a lot of them, and traffic. Good God. He began to realize what he was hearing. No... no. He felt a horrible sinking feeling slide over him. "Are you alright?" Somehow, he knew she wasn't.

Her laugh was faint, but he heard it, "Alright?" she said breathlessly and slowly, "No, I'm not alright..." Then she coughed.

"Nikki?" Please, please tell me what's going on?" He could hardly breathe, and he was listening with every fiber of his being.

"Ok. Right now," she began with an ironic lilt to her voice, "I'm pinned between what's left of my car, the guardrail, some wall." She moaned softly, "And a truck." She chuckled softly, "I think I'm going be a little late for work."

He blinked, realizing what she was saying to him. Suddenly all the background sounds were making sense, and the hair on his arms began to raise up all on their own. "Darling, listen to me, stay calm. I can hear the rescue folks there. They'll get you out." There was a pause.

"No.... well, yes, they will eventually." He heard her sob.

"Please, hang on, Nikki," he tried to speak to her in calm soothing tones as his heart pounded. "They will get you out." Of what? His mind raced uncontrollably. What the hell was going on

"No," she began breathlessly. "Listen to me. Please, I don't know how long I can..." Her voice trailed off and all he heard was the chaos in the background.

He felt the blood drain from his face, and suddenly felt chilled to the bone. He listened and hoped he could hear her over his wildly pounding heart.

She spoke slowly and deliberately, as if explaining to a child. "They gave me morphine. A lot of morphine. I want you to understand; right now I don't feel any pain."

Jesus Christ, he thought, why the hell are they letting her talk on the phone? He didn't understand. "Right Now? You're hurt? Nikki..."

"Adam, listen to me. They told me, they told me they'd get me out, but...baby, I know I'm not going to make it through this." Her voice sounded weak and breathless. "Adam, when they try to move me, I'm... I'm... I'm going to die."

He staggered backwards, his legs became weak and he could

barely stand. He wasn't hearing this; he couldn't believe he was hearing her say this. "What the hell do you mean? Why in God's name would they tell you that??" He began to feel rage; rage at what he was hearing, and rage at himself for being so helpless and so very far away from her at this moment.

"They didn't tell me that; they can't." She replied softly, patiently, "But I can tell, oh, God, I just can tell. Someone found my phone, somehow, and they told me to use it, use it while I could. The looks on their faces," she gasped again, and he could hear her breathing hard and trying not to cry. "I had to call you and tell you I love you...one last time."

"Why? He asked, "How? Why do you think that?" He tried to imagine what could be so dire a situation, and yet she could speak to him like this, so matter of fact; and how it was so like her to be this way.

"It's...the pressure. I'm pinned in here, in all this metal...there's nothing they can do...hard to breath...even now. They said they have a pressure suit here, but that it looks like I'm so caught in all this mangled..." Nikki pauses and sobs, then gasps and he hears her breathing hard. Then her voice dropped to a whisper, "Adam, I'm scared."

"Nikki, I know baby," he whispers back to her as tears well up in his eyes.

"They told me the pressure is keeping me from bleeding out," she spoke faster. "They said once they move this truck off my car, and this garbage gets taken off of me...once the pressure is released..." She paused. "I think I saw that on a TV show one time."

He blinked at the unexpected non sequitur. "Sweetheart," he said softly, a trembling smile playing across his face. "When did you ever watch TV?"

A small, breathless laugh escaped her. "Only when the internet was down," she tried to say lightly. Then she drew her breath in sharply, and in a voice that was shaking with effort continued, "They told me to call if there was someone... while they got ready." Her words flowed faster but more breathless as she rushed out, "I wanted to tell you I love you. I had to hear your voice one more time, Adam...your voice...I'll always hear...your voice."

"I love you more than life itself," he shot back passionately. "You have to know that. I would do anything for you. I'd trade places with you right now, if God would let me, Nikki. I would."

"Don't say that," she pleaded weakly with him. "I don't want to think about that." He almost choked; what did she think he was thinking about at this moment?

He stumbled to the chair by the window and sat down hard, not believing what he was hearing. Tears began to flow down his face, but he didn't notice. He felt his control slipping away, but he fought it like it was the most important fight in his life, as though somehow with his strength he could fight for her life. "This can't be true, Nikki, now try to get a hold of yourself; they have to be able...they have to have some way to help you." His voice shook as he spoke.

"They have to help me?" Her voice was tired, and she laughed thinly. "If I were a dog, they'd just push in the plunger on this morphine drip and end it now; that would help me! But no, they ethically can't do that. They have to make the effort, and they know there's just no hope. I can see it on their faces, Adam. It's how they look at me."

He hears her gasp again, and the pain he feels goes beyond anything he thought was possible to feel.

"It's so hard to breath," she said faintly.

He closes his eyes, and his voice shakes with emotion he can't control. "I love you, Nikki." He doesn't hear her at all, not even her breathing. "Nikki?"

"I love you, too, Adam." Her voice was barely a whisper now, "I always will love you. I want...I want to thank you, for trusting your instincts, too, that first day we met. I want you to remember something, Adam. Promise me, when I'm gone, I want you to .... I want you to try to live a life of happiness again. Like I did, with you...for a while. Promise me...dammit."

The words came out that she asked for, "I promise," he said weakly, not meaning a word of it. "I love you." he said again, "I love you so much." Squeezing his eyes shut he puts a hand over his face. This is isn't happening, he thinks in desperation. I'm going to tell her I'll move out there tomorrow. Job be dammed, I can find another job out there."

Rustling came through the phone's speaker, then a male voice booms through the receiver. "Sir, this is Major Thomas Dawson of the Maryland State Police." Adam's hand drops from his face, and he opens his eyes and stares unseeingly straight ahead.

The door behind him opens slowly and Steven looks into the office. Outside the door, Steven had heard enough to know there was something terrible going on with this phone call. When he sees his friend's condition, he quietly slips unnoticed into the office and stands back by the door near the corner in silent companionship.

"Sir...?" the voice on the phone says again.

"Yes sir, I'm here." Adam said tonelessly.

"Sir, I have to ask, are you her significant other, or in some way related to the vic....lady?"

He put his hand over his eyes again, fighting for control. Victim, the officer had almost said. Past tense. My God, it is true, the officer has confirmed that she is as good as dead already. Nausea warred with shock as both threatened to engulf him, but he somehow manages to hold them at bay. Adam realizes the officer was waiting for him to respond. His voice shakes as he simply replied to the officer with one word. "Yes." "Officer," Adam asked quickly, before he asks him more direct questions. "She says, she seems to believe that she's going to die. Just what the hell is going on there?"

The officer considered the question, and hesitated, debating the wisdom of describing the scene before him. Well, the officer thought, if I was in that poor bastard's shoes, I'd want to know. The Major sighed and said, "I'm not supposed to recount events at the scene of an accident before filing a report, Sir, but to be honest, if I were you, I'd want to know. What happened here was a multi-vehicle collision involving a tractor trailer and at least three other vehicles. It seems the semi was changing lanes, and had a blowout It apparently veered across two lanes, taking several cars through the guardrail and into the sound barrier with it. The wreckage is extensive, and Sir, so is the damage…" The officer's voice trailed off to silence.

Adam stared at the wall in front of him, visualizing what the officer had said, and even more significantly, what he hadn't said. Another chill crept over his body as he fought away the mental images that tried to appear. He schooled his voice as best he could, but it still trembled despite his efforts. "Officer, when are they going to get her out of there?"

The officer replied steadily, "The rescue personnel have been preparing the site to make any extraction attempt as safe as possible considering the circumstances. There's a lot of gear and equipment assembled here in very tight quarters. The debris has to be stabilized as best it could be before any extrication attempt is made. The same can be said for Ms. Anderson; the medical personnel have done," the officer pauses, then stoically said, "They've done what they can for her, Sir."

"Done what they can," Adam whispered, "Attempt?" He snapped at the officer, "Extraction attempt, what the hell is that supposed to mean?

"Sir," the officer's voice was firm but not unsympathetic, "My understanding is that Ms. Anderson's internal injuries are extensive, and her condition is grave. The rescue team personnel present have relayed to me that when the extraction is attempted, there will likely be sudden and dramatic loss of blood pressure caused by probable catastrophic internal hemorrhaging. She is as stable and as comfortable now as they could possibly make her, Sir." The officer took a breath, "I am sorry, Sir." The implications were inescapable, and so was the weight of grief that began to enshroud him.

"Sir," the officer continued, "could I get your name please? We're trying to tell from her contact list on her cell phone who should be called and, do you know, does she have any other next of kin?"

Adam shudders as he hears that phrase of finality. Taking a deep breath, he answers with a voice raspy and deep with emotion. "Her daughters; she has two daughters. Julia and Carol."

Major Dawson sighed and replied, "We called the numbers listed for those names. We got voicemail. We have other people trying to call them repeatedly so she can... say her goodbyes if we can reach them in time."

Adam looked up at the ceiling. "My God in heaven!" he thought with disbelief. "This is real, isn't it? Nikki is going to die?" He wanted to run; he wanted to scream. His calm was devolving into panic. Panic at holding back premature grief.

The calm deep voice of the officer once again jerked Adam back to the unpleasant present. The Major inquired in a somber tone, "Sir, just where are you? Maybe we can send an escort."

Adam swallowed hard before he could form the words. "Denver, Colorado."

He heard the Major swear quietly under his breath, "Goddamn." Then more loudly, "I'm sorry Sir, I truly am." Adam heard the officer take a deep breath. "I had to ask Sir, I had to know if there was a chance you could get here before," The officer tried to distract the man on the other end of the phone. He could see what Adam could not. "before they tried to extract her. The lady, Ms. Anderson, has been very brave. In fact, she's worried because we're holding up traffic, and keeping all the rescue workers here."

Adam blinked rapidly; his tears unnoticed by him have already soaked the front of his shirt. "Officer, could I please speak with Nikki again?"

Suddenly a horrendously loud sound in the background drowns out the reply of the officer. It was the mind numbing and unbelievably chilling sound of stressed metal groaning and giving way, then the sound of metal screeching against metal before finally crashing to a halt. It was silent for a second, then Adam heard people begin yelling and giving orders. He could hear their footsteps running in the background, and all the general sounds of chaos, and at that moment, Adam knew. He didn't need to hear the officer tell him. It was over, and she was gone.

Steven stared in horror at Adam. He could hear the sounds coming from the phone. He saw his friend suddenly jump to his feet, then saw Adam as he closed his eyes, his free hand clenching into a fist. After an eternity of silence, Steven heard his friend speak very quietly for a few more minutes, including hearing him telling someone his contact information. Watching Adam silently and with a growing understanding of the tragedy he was just a witness to, Steven saw his friend drop his cell on the desk.

His cell phone had skittered across the smooth surface of his desk, coming to rest against a picture frame. The impact turned the picture so Stephen could see it. It was one he had emailed Adam long ago. It was of Adam and Nikki in the Plaza, and they were dancing.

Steven walked quickly to Adam's side; one look at his friend's face riddled with devastation and pain told him all he needed to know. He put his hand on Adam's shoulder as Adam slowly surrendered to his grief.

It rained hard the night before. The air smelled fresh and was laced with the scent of honeysuckle and clover. The early morning dew clung to everything in sight, and the sunlight that peeked through the clouds turned the droplets clinging everywhere into prisms that sparkled like diamonds strewn on the grass. Adam got out of the rental car and looked up the hill, then began to walk toward the mountain of fresh flowers he saw there. He didn't need to ask directions or guess where to go. He had been here yesterday.

Michael Anderson was engraved on the black granite. Nothing more. Nothing more was needed to tell Adam that what his heart yearned for so desperately was forever laid to rest under that mountain of flowers at his feet. He knew one day soon they'd move that headstone out of there, and her name would be engraved on it alongside Michael's. He knew he could never bear to see that. He doubted he'd ever be able to come here again.

Adam's throat was dry, and his heart beat a dirge to suit his silent agony. He stared at the flowers for a long time. Then he raised his eyes slowly back to the headstone and looked again at Michael's name. Through a melancholy grin, Adam's voice was soft and accusing. "You won. She's with you now." He thought of more to say, but his voice failed him. Adam walked closer to the flowers and knelt on one knee. His right hand reached down and touched the wet and muddy ground under the flowers. How cold the soil felt to his touch. He remembered her saying how much she hated the cold, and Adam bowed his head as grief overcame him.

He had no idea how long he had remained in that position, thinking of her, wishing he had done more, sooner. He thought about all the could haves and would haves that now were just empty and unfulfilled promises. They left a bitter taste in his mouth. "I didn't lie to you, Nikki." Adam whispered, "but, this…this happened before …" his voice trailed off to silence. The only thing that pulled him away from his thoughts was the sound of car doors closing nearby.

Adam stood up and brushed the now dry mud off his hands. He looked toward the road and saw Nikki's daughters walking toward him. He blinked back tears and looked back down at the flowers. God, they looked so much like her. They wordlessly walked up to him and touched him on his arm and shoulder in silent commiseration. Adam couldn't speak to them; if he tried to say one word now, he knew he'd fall apart.
Julia noticed, and silently linked her arm through his. Carol looked at his face appraisingly, as if daring him to cry. Then Carol opened her

purse, pulled something out and handed it to Adam. He looked at it, then back at Carol wordlessly.

"Adam," Carol said quietly, "take this, please." He gently took the iPod from her, and then looked back to Carol with his question silently written across his face. Carol sighed and looked at Julia.

It was Julia who spoke for them both. "We decided…we wanted you to have that." Julia sniffed, and looked up at Adam's face. "It was Mom's." That was all she could say before her bottom lip started to quiver and she looked back down at the flowers.

Carol then spoke, her voice almost a whisper. "Adam," she said softly, and inwardly he cringed; both the girls voices sounded like hers, but Carol more so of the two. Carol waited until Adam could look at her before she continued. "Everything that was our Mom, is in there. Every song she ever sang, every story she ever wrote. All her pictures, screenshots from her games, and her emails to and from you, all of it is on there."

Adam looked down at what was in his hand and felt a wave of anguish wash over him. All he could do was shake his head in the negative. He couldn't take this away from her daughters.

Before he could voice his thoughts, Carol touched his hand and smiled a little before she spoke. "It's not like we don't have all of this already. We just thought you'd…well, we just thought you should have it. We want you to, because it's a way for her to be with you." Carol then looked down at the flowers and affirmed to him in a voice that was barely a whisper, "She loved you."

CHAPTER VI

Gasping for air, Adam sprang bolt upright in bed. It was dark, still night, and his senses reeled as he tried to get his bearings. He fumbled for the lamp on the nightstand and managed to knock it over. Heart hammering, he looked in the direction of the sound and in doing so saw the clock. It was 3:30 in the morning.

He groaned, reached down and grabbed the lamp, turned it on, then set it back on the nightstand. He could feel the sheets around him were drenched with sweat, as he had been, and as his damp skin was exposed to the air, he began to feel the night chill. He looked back at the clock with distain, 3:30 in the morning. He stopped and sadly considered the irony. He looked toward the living room and paused. It was dark out there except for the city's night-lights as they played across the walls.

Adam got out of bed and stripped it of the damp bed sheets and tossed them aside. Then he went to the linen closet and took out a fresh set and remade his bed. He wouldn't be getting back into it tonight. He walked into the bathroom and turned on the water in the shower. When the water was hot enough, he stepped inside. He put his hand on the tile and leaned on it, letting the hot water run over his body, warming and relaxing him.

He didn't know how much longer he could take this; the feeling never went away, not entirely. He knew what he had to do; what he needed to do. In a way he acknowledged that it was indeed too early, but he knew she'd understand. He finished up in the shower, stepped out and toweled himself off. He walked through the dark living room into the kitchen and put some coffee on, then went back to the bedroom and got dressed. Then he walked into the living room and towards his computer table.

The computer table had its own lamp, and Adam snapped that on as he sat down in the chair at the table. He booted up his machine and as it situated itself, he reached for his cell phone and touched a speed dial number without looking at his phone. He pulled a cigarette out of the pack that was in front of him and lit it; he hoped she'd forgive him for what he was about to do.

The phone rang about eight times before he heard the line come alive, and he heard a sleepy, familiar voice. "Hello?"

"Hello, darling." he said warmly.

"Adam, is that you?"

He smiled sheepishly even though no one was there to see him. "Hello Nikki, yes, it's Adam." He heard her move around, and the faint click of a lamp on her end of the phone.

"Adam, are you alright?" Nikki asked in a fuzzy voice.

"Yes, baby, I'm ok...well... as ok as I can be without you with me."

Nikki crooned into the phone. "Aww, that's so sweet. But Adam, you know it's 6AM here, right?"

Adam chuckled, "Yes, darling. I'm so sorry to wake you. I hope you can forgive me; I just had to call you." He shrugged to himself. "I needed to hear your voice, and I had to know that you're ok."

Nikki paused, and knew something was up with Adam. If he needed to call her at this hour, something must have happened. She got a feeling of dread and imagined wild confessions of wonton sessions of sex with college girls, and then she smiled at that visual. Yeah, right. "Adam, what's wrong? she asked him directly, "and don't even try to tell me nothing is; I doubt you'd have called me and woke me up just to say hi."

Adam sighed and grinned into the darkness. "Lady, you know me so well." he chuckled softly, "Well, I did call you to prove to myself that you were alright, and to just hear your voice." Adam took a drag on his cigarette before continuing, "Nikki, I had a dream, a horrible nightmare to be exact. When I woke up and looked at the clock, it said 3:30." He waited and was rewarded with the anticipated chuckle from her. "So, you do understand, I had to call you."

"Yes, Adam, I understand." Nikki smiled fondly at the time reference; she could understand that perfectly. "So, Adam." Nikki carefully asked, "What was the nightmare about?"

"No, I'm not going to tell you about it; at least not now. You still need to get some sleep, and besides," he stalled, "it's too fresh in my mind for me to go over it with you now."

"Damn, that must have been something pretty bad, huh?" Nikki was trying to draw him out.

Adam knew she was going to try to wheedle him into telling her, so he decided to end that notion now. "Nikki, suffice it to say, it was bad enough to have me up, wide awake and even showered and dressed at this hour. Not to mention bad enough to call you at 6AM just to placate myself by hearing your voice."

Nikki nodded to herself in affirmation; there would be no getting it out of him tonight. "But what about you, Adam? You said you're showered and dressed; sounds to me like you're ready to go to work. You won't be going back to sleep either."

"Either?" Adam picked up on that and smiled softly. "My love, I am going to hang up in a few minutes, and you're going to try to go back to sleep. I'm sorry I woke you up, and I do feel awful that I did, but... Well, not too awful," he laughed quietly. "I really did need to hear your voice." He needed more than that, and he intended to begin working on that some more when he hung up. Adam smiled to himself knowing what he was working on. "And again, you are correct. I do have some things here I need to work on; might as well do it now while it's quiet before I go into the office."

"You're gonna be tired later." Nikki scolded.

"Yes, dear." Adam acquiesced. "But I can come home and take a nap when I'm done; you can't exactly do that. So, go back to bed and sleep, my love. I love you, Nikki." Adam waited.

"I love you too, Adam, you big mushball."

Smiling, but not disagreeing, Adam said softly, "I'll talk to you later. Goodnight, baby."

"Goodnight, darling," Nikki said, and then she hung up.

Adam always waited and let her hang up first, just in case she might want to say one more thing. He put his cell phone in the pocket of his shirt and looked at his monitor. He opened the document he wanted to work on, then he got up and went to the kitchen to warm up his coffee. Walking to the window, he recalled the second night Nikki was here, when he saw her by the window silhouetted by these very lights. He looked at the couch and loveseat where they talked, and did other things, for hours. He smiled at both memories.

Then not surprisingly, he remembered his dream; how vivid and horrifyingly real it had seemed to him. He didn't usually dream; not ones he remembered anyway. He thought about how Steven making an appearance in it; now that was odd. But upon consideration, no it wasn't, really. Steven did give him the time he needed to be with her. Adam scoffed, not that he wouldn't have taken the time anyway, but Steven had no intention of denying him that opportunity. Steven was willing to help and even to push, if it came down to that, because he was all too familiar with Adam's stubbornness. And, he did send those pictures to him; pictures that they sent to Nikki's crazy friend Anna. Pictures that he looked at every day.

He grinned and sipped his coffee again. Some of those pictures had even shown up on the bulletin board at work in the break room. He hoped Jonathan was happy, wherever he was working now. Not that he fired him; the thought never entered his mind. However, Jonathan did seem a bit uncomfortable at work after that day. It might have had something to do with the fact that all the employees had made it their mission in life to give Jonathan no end of grief about that day in the Plaza. They never missed a chance to remind him about being so stupid as to hit on the boss's girlfriend and right in front of him, no less, and therefore negating all his stories about being such a Don Juan.

Then there was the reference to Ingwa International. Adam walked back to his computer table and sat down, looking at the proposal he was working on. He hesitated, and then logged into his network account for work. He accessed the project planner, and sure enough, there was a potential meeting scheduled with Ingwa, but it was six months away. He tapped the desk with a pen. Oh, of course, it seemed so familiar because they had a budget meeting recently. Adam narrowed his eyes, they surely did, and the topic of travel did come up.

As Adam put his feet up on the desk, he recalled discussing with Steven who should go to Japan, and yes, they did talk about having a videoconference. Adam's pet project was videoconferencing and telecommuting. The way their firm was growing and expanding toward both coasts, it only made sense. He was a firm believer that if someone was worth their salt, they would do their job better if they were comfortable. If working at home suited his people, then he was all for it. They'd hang themselves soon enough if their work wasn't completed to his satisfaction, and then if forced to they'd be chained to a desk. That was company policy, but not his. He personally didn't agree with that philosophy. He always felt that if someone had to be watched and be in one spot in order to be productive, then they really weren't the kind of talent he'd prefer to have working for him. There was trust, and then, there wasn't. No middle ground allowed on that topic.

That made him think of Nikki again, and what had happened in this very chair months ago. It was a bittersweet memory. Trust. It was kind of the same type of trust, so there was a connection. Trusting in someone's intentions when you can't see them, or be with them, or watch over them. In one sense, he had that relationship with his people at work, and in a very different but similar sense, he and Nikki experienced that type of trust. This reminded him, when he finally did meet Anna, he owed her a word or two about her lack of tact and sensitivity.

Adam's eyes roamed back to the schedule again; there was something else he had talked to Steven about, but he couldn't put his finger on it. He scanned the schedule again, wondering what he might be missing. His eye kept coming back to the videoconferencing.

"I wonder…" Adam mused aloud. His feet came off the tabletop and hit the floor with a thud. Could it be this fucking simple? He chuckled sardonically to himself. Well, why the hell not? He should kick himself for not thinking of it sooner. Nikki would cheerfully help him, too. Adam laughed. "Talk about not seeing the forest for the trees," he admonished himself aloud. He went back to the document he originally had sought to work on and began editing it wholesale. He just had his epiphany; now to see if he could make it look as good on paper as it sounded in theory.

Steven looked at his watch; Adam would be coming in here in five minutes. When he arrived this morning, there was both an email and a voicemail from Adam asking if he could squeeze in fifteen minutes for him today. Hell, for Adam, he could squeeze in whatever he asked for; the man never asked him for much at all. He couldn't be happier with a right-hand man than he was with Adam. It wasn't that he was such a workaholic; it was more that he knew when to work, and when to play. Steven had to chuckle. Being in love didn't hurt Adam's productivity one bit. Adam was simply, well rounded and more balanced now. If anything, it made him more focused, more creative on the job if that was even possible.

He heard a knock on his open door. No surprise, Adam was early. "Good morning, Adam. How's it going today?" Steven greeted him warmly.

Adam strode in and reached across the desk, as they shook hands, Adam said, "Not too bad, sir, and how about you? How's the baby doing?"

Steven pulled out his wallet, looking a bit self-conscience. Adam laughed and then motioned encouragingly, "Common, let me see them." Steven showed Adam the newest baby pictures and Adam had to admit, he was a pudgy little cutie.

"Nikki have any kids, Adam?" Steven asked conversationally as he tucked his wallet back into his pants pocket. Adam sat down in one of the chairs in front of Steven's desk and he nodded. "Two daughters, they're in their mid-twenties I believe."

Steven did a double take, and Adam tried not to notice. "You're shitting me," Steven said incredulously, "Well, damn, did she have them at very young age?"

Adam shook his head in the negative, and stoically said, "Steven, Nikki is only one year younger than I am."

Steven whistled quietly. "Is that so," Steven teased his sometimes too serious friend and co-worker. "And here we were thinking you robbed the cradle."

Adam's eyebrows raised a bit. That's all the answer Steven was going to get, and he knew it. Adam wasn't uptight, he just was the consummate gentleman, so discussing the lady's age and when she had her children, and perhaps reminding him of the father of those children might not have been the best way to start off this meeting. To attempt to make amends, Steven offered, "Well, obviously, time has been good to her."

"Speaking of time," Adam stood up, and placed the proposal on Steven's desk so he could read the header, "how soon do you think we can make this happen?"

Steven looked at the package and read aloud the top line on the cover page of the proposal. "East Coast Regional Manager?" Steven looked back up at Adam quizzically. "We don't have an East Coast Regional Manager."

Adam leaned forward, placing his hands-on Steven's desk, and grinned. "We will, if you approve that proposal."

Steven grunted, then started to thumb through the pages and spoke as he scanned the document. "Well, I know we're growing like wildfire, more so to the east coast than the west, this is true," Steven's voice trailed off. "You know, this might be just the time to do this, take control and have some guidance in place for our expansion goals. Knowing you," Steven shut the proposal and folded his hands-on top of it. "I'm sure all the details have been vetted by you to my satisfaction. I always trust your instincts, Adam."

Adam had to use all his self-control to keep his expression from changing when he heard that phrase come out of Steven's mouth.

"This actually may not be a bad idea to implement right now, Adam. We'd have to put out a vacancy announcement that will cover our entire target area. Have you given thought to what vehicle might be best?"

"Actually, no Steven," Adam said, removing his hands from the desk in front of him and straightening his posture. "I'm thinking more along the lines of someone in house."

"Really?" Steven opened the proposal again and looked through it some more, then he looked up at Adam and asked, "Who do you have in mind?"

Adam said without hesitation, "Me."

Steven looked up at his friend, then back at the proposal. Then he looked searchingly at Adam's face. "You're serious, aren't you?"

"Serious as a heart attack." Adam replied with a straight face.

Steven reopened the proposal. "There's not a huge budget in here, Adam..."

"We don't need a big one, sir. At first, all I'd need is office space. As I gather the threads of our growth and see who lands where, and how many we're talking about incorporating into our team, space can then be reassessed. But the immediate need is simple and clean. One office," Adam said, "mine."

"We'd have to maintain our working relationship as it is, though. There'd be a lot of travel involved, Adam."

"That's not how I see it, sir. I could make one trip per month back here to Denver, more or less, if need be, but I can be in touch at any time via video, or teleconference. I foresee no difficulty whatsoever communicating with the home office here, or anywhere else we need to do business. This is exactly the business model we've been discussing for our future. Might as well implement it now."

Steven grunted, stood up and carried the proposal to the window, reading parts of it, and scanning the rest.

Adam was rooted to the ground where he stood, outwardly composed. Inside his guts were in turmoil; this was going far better than he hoped.

Steven looked out the window, his voice became low and quiet. "You must think I'm the dumbest ass you've ever met, don't you Adam?"

That drew a surprised gasp out of Adam. He felt his heart sink. "Sir?" Adam then said in shock, "Pardon me?

Steven looked out the window a moment more in silence and then turned to look at his friend. Steven's demeanor was all business. "This is one hell of a good idea. It's timely, cost conscious, and probably is something that will give our company a real boot in the ass. I can only imagine that you'd want to suggest that the office might be in, oh, perhaps somewhere in the D.C. metro area; for some odd reason that jumps to the front of my mind. And I have to agree, you'd be the perfect person to head the team, here, out west, or even on the east coast. But Adam," Steven said reproachfully and shook his head. "To use our company as a tool in order to get yourself moved closer to the woman you love? I have to say, I'm ashamed." Steven's face slowly broke into the smile of an angel, "...that I didn't think of this myself." Steven held out his hand to the nonplussed Adam, "Congratulations, and welcome aboard, Mr. East Coast Regional Manager."

Adam took Steven's hand and shook it in a daze. "Thank you, Steven." Adam's voice was even, but his eyes were dancing.

Steven laughed and thumped Adam on the shoulder. "As much as you've done for this company, it's about time the company can do something for you in return. I can have this finalized with Accounting in less than two days, Adam. The numbers aren't huge. That means you can likely sign a contract for office space by the end of the week, so..." Steven grinned, "I suppose you better go out east and find that suitable office space, huh?"

Adam blinked at Steven and finally started to smile.

"We can ship anything you need out to you when you're ready for it, but I want that office opened in two weeks and not a day later." The two men stood there, smiling at each other. "So, Adam," Steven sat back down at his desk, gesturing toward the door. "I suggest you move your ass."

A.F.K.

CHAPTER VII

Anna walked back to Nikki's office down the hall and peeked in the door.

Nikki looked up and over a huge bunch of roses on her desk. "Hey, Anna." she said idly.

Anna came into the office carrying her jacket and purse; it was almost time to go home. She smelled the roses, and then sat down. "Those are just gorgeous. How many is that, two dozen?"

"I believe so," Nikki answered, and then grinned at Anna, "I didn't count them."

Anna looked at her and scoffed, "You don't need to; it's not how many there are," Anna leaned closer and whispered conspiratorially, "it's why did he send so many."

"What?" Nikki said, distracted from her work. Ok, now she has to pay attention to Anna, so she turns from her email and faces her friend and sometimes antagonist. Nikki smiled at the roses and looked at Anna with a resigned but amused expression. "Ok, why do you think he sent so many, Anna? I know you're just dying to share."

Anna looked with exaggerated pity at Nikki and patted her hand. "You really don't want to hear this."

"Oh, but I do," Nikki countered. "I need a good laugh."

Anna threw Nikki a look, and said, "Ok, I'll tell you what I think, but don't get pissed at me."

Nikki raised her eyebrows, and thought, this is gonna be good. "No promises, Anna." Nikki grinned. "But I will try not to hurt you." She picked up a pencil, and added, "Much." Nikki began twirling the pencil in her fingers, and Anna started to get up. "Ok, ok," Nikki motioned to a chair, "sit down and tell me."

Anna glanced at the pencil twirling in Nikki's fingers and

replied, "You're already pissed off."

Nikki laughed and said, "Anna, when you walk in here with sage advice, it's usually wrong, and hilarious to hear, so please tell me."

Anna should have left, but it just wasn't in her to walk away from giving Nikki a good scare now and then. Anna felt it was for Nikki's own good that she played devil's advocate, because Nikki wasn't going to allow herself to see the downside of anything that had to do with Adam. Anna gestured at the flowers. "Do you have any idea how expensive these are?" Anna had served her first volley.

"No, not really." Nikki said.

Anna laughed quietly. "A bloody fortune, that's what they cost, and roses like those? Probably at least two hundred dollars."

"Impressive." Nikki replied, and then Anna pounced. "So just why would he do that, unless he was guilty about something?"

Nikki rolled her eyes. "Jesus, Anna, tell me again, what age were you when your Mother dropped you on your head?" Nikki turned back to her email.

"Nicole, look at me. I'm serious." Anna hissed at her friend, trying to get her attention.

Nikki turned her attention back to Anna. "Anna, Adam is serious, too. As serious about me as I am about him."

Anna started with her lecturing voice, "In my experience…"

"Oh boy," Nikki cut her off. "You need to come to battle better equipped than that, Anna."

Anna just blew that off and went on, "When a man sends you something like that, he's hiding something. Or even worse, he's feeling guilty about doing something and you probably will never know what it was, because he damn sure isn't ever going to tell you about it." Anna nodded her head in self-satisfaction.

With concern and frustration, Nikki said quietly, "Why do you do this to me, Anna? Why do you walk in here every other day and come up with the most outlandish shit imaginable, and try to make me believe it about Adam? Is there a website you get this from, because if there is, I'm going to call IT and have that IP address banned from our network."

With sympathy in her voice, Anna responded. "Outlandish? Me? You and him, that's the very definition of outlandish. This long-distance romance garbage is total bullshit, Nikki. It's not going to work, I mean, how long has it been? Five months now, six months you've been mooning over this phantom. And, you really have not one bit of assurance, other than what he tells you, that he's as faithful to you as are you are to him."

Nikki looked at Anna and gave due consideration to what she said. "It's been six months, to the day." Nikki gestured toward the flowers, "Hence the flowers. They're from Adam, for our six-month anniversary."

Anna looked subdued for a moment, but then she thought she saw a flash of doubt in Nikki's eyes, so she pounced. "I just want you to think, Nikki. I don't want to see him, or anyone else hurt you." Anna put her hand on Nikki's wrist again. "Haven't you been hurt enough, girl? First you lose your husband, and then, miracle of miracles, when you do fall in love with a man again, he's not even around? Think, girl, both the men you love, and neither one will ever be here with you. Why do you do this to yourself?"

Nikki stared at Anna; comparing the two vastly different situations was just too damn much, even for Anna's uniquely warped mind. She chose to be reasonable and not appear offended, but the effort was costing her in patience. "That's life, Anna, we can't control everything that happens to us." Nikki took a deep breath trying to maintain her patience. "Nor can we control how we feel."

"You can't control how often you see him, either, can you, Nikki?" Anna countered. "Let's keep it to the facts, not what you want, or what he tells you he wants." Anna was on a roll now. "In the past six months, how many times have you seen Adam? No, wait," Anna grabbed the small calculator from Nikki's desk.

Nikki huffed the answer at Anna, her irritation growing by the minute. "You know damn well, Anna. It was when I went to Denver, and then I met him in Florida two months ago."

Anna tapped the keys on the calculator. "Ok, that was for three days, so…" Anna grabbed Nikki's pencil out of her fingers and started tabulating numbers. Anna muttered out loud as she scribbled. "Six months, one hundred eighty days; of which you saw him for five in Denver, and three in Florida."

Nikki scowled. "I get your point, Anna."

"That's eight days out of one hundred and eighty. Eight days with him, as opposed to one hundred and seventy two days without him in the last six months." Anna looked up at Nikki with sympathy in her eyes. "Nikki, honey, I see my dentist more often than that." Anna put the calculator back on Nikki's desk. "I'll spare you the breakdown in hours."

Nikki snatched the pencil from Anna, broke it in half, and threw it the trash can under her desk, and told Anna heatedly, "That's only because you can't figure out the formula for the math, Anna, because if you could, you'd shove that figure up my ass, too."

Anna's eyebrows shot upwards in mock horror. "Nikki! You never told me you were into that!"

Nikki didn't laugh. She looked at the clock behind her; it

was 5:30. She got up and started to gather her things to go home, and she told Anna icily, "It's a good thing for you I need to go home now." She picked up her purse and briefcase, brushed past Anna, and walked out of her office. The footsteps behind her followed her all the way to the elevator, but she didn't look to see who it was; she knew it was Anna. The elevator arrived and Nikki got in with Anna on her heels.

Nikki refused to look at her, but Anna had one more question. "Nikki," Anna asked quietly. "Did Adam call you today? Or for that matter, since he left on this trip?" Nikki looked up at Anna through veiled eyes and answered flatly, "No."

The elevator opened, and they both walked out the building's front door toward the parking garage. Nikki just kept walking, not even looking at Anna, let alone talking to her. Finally, Anna spoke in a conciliatorily way. "Ok, maybe he is tied up in meetings; you know, busy working."

Nikki looks sidelong at Anna and scoffs. "Of course, he is, Anna. I know Adam; he will call when he can."

Anna just can't let Nikki be so blasé and naive about what she sees as danger signals. "Ok, but what if something did happen, and he's with someone else? What if he's not really traveling and he just doesn't want you calling while he's with her? Do you honestly think he would tell you?"

Nikki abruptly grabs Anna's arm, pulling her over with her as she detours out of the flow of pedestrian traffic and onto a little grassy picnic area that borders the sidewalk. In a tone of steel that makes even Anna blink, Nikki leans forward and hisses, "Look. I am so tired of you…"

The sound of Nikki's cell phone ringing stops her mid-sentence. As Nikki reaches into her bag to retrieve her phone, she continues to stare at Anna in silent and restrained fury.

Anna knows that ring tone, and rolls her eyes, but deep down inside she's glad the guy called her; and also is grateful that the timing of the call saved her from one royal ass chewing.

Staring with annoyance at Anna, Nikki answers with a melancholy voice. "Hey, Adam."

"Hello, Nikki, how are you?"

Nikki can't help but smile when she hears his voice. "I'm doing ok, I guess. Oh, and thank you for the flowers. They're beautiful."

"And so are you! Happy anniversary, baby! I'm glad you like them. I, however, love you very much."

Nikki sighed, not sure what to say next. "I love you too, Adam. Happy anniversary to you, too."

Anna couldn't stand it and pantomimed sticking her finger

down her throat and started making quiet gagging noises at Nikki, who waved at her to be quiet.

"Ask him where he is." Anna whispered with urgency. Nikki looked at Anna with daggers and turned away from her.

"Nikki, you sound down. Are you feeling ok?" Adam's voice was laced with concern.

"I'm ok, a bit sad, you know how that is… I miss you." She laughed a small nervous laugh.

"Yes, my love," Adam said ruefully. "I do know exactly how that is, and I promise you I intend to change that, and very, very soon."

Nikki sighs again. Even she grows weary of hearing that sometimes, and after what Anna had to say it wasn't what Nikki wanted to hear. "I know, we're both trying." Nikki leaves it at that. She doesn't want Anna to know for sure that she's been scoping out jobs closer to Denver, but she has a feeling that she already suspects.

Anna smirks at the phone and shrugs.

Now Nikki must know where Adam is, and she mentally curses Anna and her big mouth. "Listen, Adam," Nikki begins tentatively. "Yesterday afternoon when we were talking and you told me you'd be traveling and leaving in a few hours; that trip came up rather suddenly, didn't it?" Nikki hesitated, waiting for him to answer.

"Yes, it did." Adam confirmed, "But sometimes we have to move fast. You know that." Adam couldn't help but grin. He knew he was teasing Nikki now but couldn't help himself. "Particularly when we're motivated."

Nikki frowned, wondering who "we" was, and just what could be so motivating. Did he actually forget that he didn't tell her where he was going, or was it just a memory lapse of convenience? That was hard to believe.

It didn't help to have Anna whispering behind her, "That's my girl, pin him down. Go on, ask him where he is."

Nikki draws in a breath and lets it out slowly. "Adam," Nikki goes on slowly. "You didn't tell me where you were going."

Anna gasps and puts her hand on Nikki's arm, but Nikki doesn't want her encouragement right now.

"Adam, did you hear me?" Nikki asks again.

"Yes darling, I hear you." Then nothing.

Nikki is rapidly becoming annoyed, and she's certain she wouldn't be annoyed in the least at Adam if Anna hadn't goaded her so much in the first place. Nikki says in a less that patient tone, "Well, Adam, are you going to tell me where you are or not?"

Anna is practically jumping up and down now at Nikki's side

like a demented cheerleader, and if that wasn't distracting enough, she grabs Nikki by the arm and squeals.

"Hold on a sec…" Nikki lowers the phone from her ear and hisses at her friend, who is making her insane with her jumping and squealing. "Anna, for Christ sake," Nikki snaps at her friend in exasperation. "Will you stop! I can't hear a damn thing Adam is saying! Jesus!" Nikki turns back to her cell phone and practically shouts into it, "Adam, would you mind telling me, just where in the hell are you?"

Anna tugs hard on Nikki's arm and insistently pulls her around by her sleeve.

Nikki turns and looks at Anna with annoyance and sees she is still bouncing up and down with barely contained glee. "Anna, what in the hell is wrong with you…"

Anna squeals again, puts her hands on Nikki's shoulders, and turns her around.

"Oh my God…" Nikki barely breaths out the words.

Adam is standing not ten feet in front of her with two suitcases near his feet. Adam always traveled light; with one bag of carry-on luggage at most. At least, in the past he had, Nikki thought to herself.

Casually tossing his cell into the bushes by the sidewalk, Adam smiles and strides toward her. Startled again by the audaciousness of what she just witnessed, Nikki blinks and her eyes follow the path of the discarded cell phone. "Adam, why the hell did you…?" but her question is quickly interrupted by Adam when he reaches her, pulls her into his arms and kisses her lovingly and quite thoroughly.

After what she considers to be a generous amount of time, Anna, who is standing nearby, but not too nearby, clears her throat in an exaggeratedly loud manner.

As Adam and Nikki reluctantly end their kiss, Nikki is the first to speak. "My God, Adam!" Nikki's grin gets even wider. "Adam? What are you doing here? You're here on business?"

Adam smiles happily at her, kisses her again lightly on the lips and concedes, "Well, not at this particular moment." Adam's gaze then falls upon Anna, who is looking at him expectantly. From what Nikki has told him and recalling his own brief but trying experience with Anna, he has no doubt that's he looking at trouble incarnate. With an amused voice, Adam says to Nikki, "I take it this is Anna."

Nikki, still caught up in the shock at having Adam right here in front of her, blinks and quickly states apologetically, "Oh, I'm so sorry." Nikki turns to Anna, "Adam, this is Anna Reeves; Anna, this," Nikki sighs and smiles delightedly. "This, is Adam Preston."

Anna affects an impish grin, and holds out her hand to Adam, who takes it and shakes it in a formal but friendly manner. Anna gives Adam a somewhat disappointed look, "What? No kiss for me?" Then she shoots a glance at Nikki and remarks, "Careful bastard, isn't he?"

Adam laughs and Nikki gives Anna a warning look.

Anna doesn't miss her friends glare and tossing her head, she turns to Adam and while handing him his cell phone she says mischievously, "Here you go, handsome, you must have missed your pocket." Anna must have retrieved it while she and Adam were previously somewhat occupied.

Nikki shakes her head and can't imagine why Adam did such a thing, but as she considers how to begin to ask, Adam graciously takes the phone from Anna.

"Thank you, Anna, but, I really did mean to throw it away. I won't need it anymore." he quips, his face in a deadpan expression.

Anna's eyebrows rise skyward and Nikki acquires a look that defies description, but before her look can change again, Adam continues rapidly, "I might as well get a new one, since my number will be changing. I hear from Nikki that her service provider here is pretty good." Adam then turns back to Nikki and gives her a significant look. "Maybe we can work out a joint account." A smile grows on Adam's face, then he winks at Nikki as he begins to laugh.

Nikki peers at Adam like he's lost his mind. "What? Adam, what's going on?" She stops and looks again at the luggage behind him.

"I've had a productive day." Adam began to explain, grinning as he notices where Nikki's eyes have landed. "I'm sorry I didn't call you earlier, my love, but I wanted to be sure I had this before I saw you." He reaches into his pocket, pulls out a key, and places it in Nikki's hand.

"What this?" she asks quietly, looking back from the luggage to what Adam placed in her hand.

"It's a key." Anna suggested helpfully. Nikki shot her a look that made her take a step backwards. "Ok, ok…you knew that. Sheesh."

"That," Adam interjected evenly, but with a growing smile, "is the key to our new East Coast Regional Office. I just signed the lease this afternoon." Adam pauses and lets that sink in as Nikki slowly looks from the key in her hand, to the luggage, and back to up to Adam's smiling face. Adam takes both his hands and closes them gently around the hand with which Nikki is holding the key. "It is for the office that I will start to work in as of Monday morning."

Nikki stares blankly at him and shakes her head as if to clear it; did she just hear him correctly? "What did you just say? Wait, but, for how long? Adam, when do you have to go back?"

Adam's face turns serious and he looks into her eyes.
"Except for the occasional short trip back to see the boss in Denver? Never."

Her jaw drops and Adam pulls the stunned Nikki close to him and embraces her tightly. "I'm home, Nikki," he whispers in her ear as both their eyes well up with tears of joy. "I'm home."

For once, Anna just smiles and says nothing.